A NOVEL

MARY
JAMES

ISBN 978-1-09839-608-4 (Print)
ISBN 978-1-09839-609-1 (eBook)

Disclaimer:

To my family and friends and nonfriends who read this book, you may recognize aspects, dialogue, critical events but in writing they became a composite with other fabrications. I wrote not for intellectual accuracy but for interest. If you feel left out, better luck in the next book. If you feel exposed in this book, you are only relating to traces of reality. Not one character in this book is purely you. Don't fancy yourself, please.

Both my publisher and I regret any unintentional harm from the publishing and marketing of this entirely fictional account. Note that fiction is creative and imaginative writing.

Contents

Pepper's Therapy Practice
(Rather Than a Boring Foreword)

Welcome. Please come in and choose a comfy chair. Let's get you all settled before we begin. I will dim the lights when you are ready. I see you looking at the recliner choices – Papa Bear size, Mama Bear Size and Baby Bear size. You chose the Mama Bear size, a soft creamy chenille recliner. I demonstrate how the electric foot stool raises and the back can be adjusted. Now what can we put in the cup holder for you? Diet Coke, water, tea, or coffee? Would you like a chocolate or piece of hard candy? I also have an array of sugar free candies.

I have microwaved two towels to wrap your hands in if you would like warmth. I also have a freshly laundered blanket. May I start an aromatherapy diffuser for you? I also have lavender lotion for your hands if you would like some. If you wish, I have complimentary squeeze balls and slime jars.

On your next visit, you can just help yourself to the choices on the credenza before we start our session. The goal is to relax and restore yourself in a therapeutic spa setting. Therapy doesn't have to be a grim process. Let's just sit back and when you're ready, you may start. Ah...The Pepper

Therapy Technique, characterized by kindness, hospitality, and positive regard for the client experience. Beats the heck out of Freud – right? Or those hard chairs under fluorescent lights, sitting across from some cheap motivational poster promoting "Live Your Dream". And don't get me started on the dollar store frames, hung crooked announcing the therapists' degree, in an homage to their lofty intellect and power over their clients.

Welcome to Pepper's Practice!

Chapter One
ALIVE AGAIN

"Heart" he gasped. Berry's 200 pounds slumped on me. What honey? Heart, like you heart me? You are saying you love me? Or was it fart - the gasp was so deep and raspy I am not sure. I do know that suddenly I am struggling under his weight. No fart smell, no sound. Extreme weight crushing me.

"Berry, honey, I am squished. Can you move?" There was no response.

Heart? Did Berry have a heart attack? Is a dead married man on top of me? Oh, my goodness. How do I move this giant off me? Do I call 911? Do I quickly pack my stuff and ditch this room? What can I do? He is married. And not to me. And he appears dead.

Do I know CPR? I have had 5 classes and certifications and yet my mind is blank. Rescue breathing, first? Chest compressions? Do I pump his heart five times or blow five times into his chest hair? What is that mouth thing I should do? Do I exhale five times in his mouth? Is there something I do five times? I cannot remember a thing and my own heart is hurting me.

Really hurting me. Right now, I have to get this 6'4 huge giant off me. I am 5 feet tall, and he has pinned me in the plunging position. (Don't ask me to explain the plunging position, right now. Use your imagination.) My lungs are collapsing from the compression. A numbness is creeping up from my feet.

I try to roll to the right. Berry's bowling ball head is slacked off on that side, pressing on my vocal cords. There is no movement. He is not cooperating at all. I press up and over to the left and I can't lift his head across my face. I am trapped under a naked dead man.

Think Pepper think. Use your Ph.D. and think. Useless degree. I need an advance degree in power lifting corpses. Morbid humor. But that's where my mind goes when I am scared, freaked out and beyond panicked. As I am now. Why don't cheap hotel rooms come with a Hoyer Lift – they must have men dying on top of their partners daily – right?

New idea! If I can reach my cell phone, I can call the front desk for help or 911. I try to lift his 4-foot arm towards my cell to knock it closer to me. He must really be dead because there is no resistance, just limp flesh. I try a few swipes but cannot control the motion. My own arm is only a 24-inch-long flipper and is useless.

No matter. I do not want police and EMT's unburying me to find me naked and dripping Berry goo. Not to mention the intimacy on display of a prominent, small-town businessman. Married. But not to the wench under his loins.

What am I going to do? It has been at least 10 minutes of deadness. So much for worrying if I knew CPR. At 64 years old Berry is dead from having the best sex of his life. At least I hope it was for him. Up to this dead part, it had been the best version of alpha rutting, long-distance flirting and fantasizing come true. At many points in the last 12 hours of passion, and mutual admiration and disbelief at our magnetic connection, I had the word love in my mind.

Berry spoke the word "heart". I am sure he was choking out "heart attack". Not "my heart, my soul is yours". And of course, now he never will.

Movement!!! Now he has retracted from one part of me, wink, wink but the problematic dead weight of him is creating a crisis for my breathing.

I cannot die under him and have my reputation, my family's love, and respect for me damaged. How would the headlines read? Marriage therapist found dead under married man. Suffocated by fresh corpse, immobilized by weight of lover, therapist dies for ill-begotten love. "Sex Therapy" kills local man and therapist.

Oh, the consequences will be devastating. I simply must at least get him off me and then start damage management. I try again shifting right and left. Now there is no feeling in my legs. I have spinal stenosis and this position must be pinching some major nerves. If I lose sensation in my shoulders, there will be nothing left to power Berry off me. Except for a miracle.

And so, I pray. Dear God. I know I have sinned. Super badly. Sex outside of wedlock. Sex with a married man. Sex without a condom – oh wait, that's a sin against society. Berry was Baptist – Catholics think that is a sin. Sex with Berry knowing he had a wife of 42 years. Check, that is a sin. I am such a sinner, and I chose to entertain the devil for the past year with all the flirting, sex-texting and then the culmination to this.

God, can you please help get Berry off me? I promise I will do major contrition. I am getting dizzy from his cement head crushing on me and his torso squishing my internal organs. Please?

Mary, Mother of God, don't look at my nakedness, but please ask God for mercy on my behalf. Mary - you have been so miraculous in my life. I need a miracle now. Guardian Angel please round up fifty unemployed angels and lift this poor man off me. Please, heavenly bodies - someone help me!

I start saying a rosary. After the first decade of the rosary, I try again. I push with my shoulders towards the right. Fifty angels push with me. Berry sludges off. I am free to breathe. Thank you, God, thank you Mary and thank you Guardian Angel and your friends.

I reach for my phone to call 911. Berry has not taken a breath in over 20 minutes. I lay my head on his chest to check for any rise. No rise. No breath. Berry is truly dead. And so is his reputation and mine.

I shower and change ninja fast while I wait for the police. I place a hand towel over Berry's beloved trouser snake. It was one of a kind, I assure you. Of course, without sounding like a slut who has seen thousands, it was in my limited experience. Tears flood my eyes.

There is no image management. I think God wants me to be truthful as part of my contrition.

The police enter eager to be titillated at the scene. I am Dr. Pepper James. Marriage and Family Therapist, self- employed with a lovely practice – now on the verge of being destroyed. I am 62 years old. I weigh 192 pounds. I do not live in this town of Dublin, Georgia. I am here visiting Berry. This was our first meeting after a year of playing online Scrabble. No, I do not meet every Scrabble player and have sex with them, but how sensitive of you to ask Officer Jack A. Hole.

Do you have Berry's driver's license? I fetch Berry's shorts with the lopsided heaviness from his wallet. Well, here is his wallet. I may have spread my cellulite bubbled legs but going through his wallet seems too personal. You can open it. You, the Officer with the conservative, religious crucifix up your…excuse me. Contrition correction. Please Officer, you look. I am just a weak woman, and you are a powerful soldier of law and order.

The ambulance and EMT's have arrived. Such a lovely scene – cops going through my suitcases looking for drugs, penis-enhancers, bondage equipment. I am delighted that they have discovered two packages of women's disposable underwear. Yes, those stretchy, size XL diapers really are sexy. My size 16 sundresses are such a turn on too. My makeup bag has assorted tweezers because my chin hairs are so difficult to pull out, I need an arsenal of weapons.

No perfume. No sexy lingerie. My anti-depressant is the only drug. No expensive jewelry. No pornographic materials. No handcuffs or French Maid outfits. No high heels because my knees are arthritic, and I wear orthopedic shoes. My walker is hidden in the closet because I didn't want Berry to see it. My life is truly the opposite of a sex starved kitten, clearly.

But for one glorious dalliance with Berry, I managed to be my former self – a passionate woman.

The hotel room's two wastebaskets are taken by a junior Barney Fife character who has a leering smirk on his face. Oh, to see that smirk disappear when he has to search the wastebasket looking for an empty Viagra box, pot brownie wrapper, or disposable dildo and finds instead several massively heavy pairs of disposable underwear soaked with my very own urine, black mascara tipped Q-tips, wrappers from diet bars, couple tissues with dead palmetto cockroach carcasses, remnant of a sundress I let Berry rip off my body, semen-soaked cloths, and a paper towel with road runner brown streaks. Have fun itemizing those items Barney!

Finding nothing of prurient interest, everyone is packing to leave. There is a dead man who needs an extra-long stretcher and more men to carry him out, but nothing else. Officer Jack A Hole addresses me. Come to the station to complete some paperwork. You can ride in my car.

May I take my rental car please? I will follow you. If you think I will flee – you can keep my disposable underwear in your car. I don't go anywhere without them – seriously.

I have done the maximum amount of damage to Berry. His wife has been contacted. She knows he died on top of a woman from Minnesota. His 42 years of marriage has been destroyed. Soon Berry's daughter will know. Daddy – the Southern daddy – went from hero to hellion in one phone call.

I am returning to Minnesota, to my practice, to my eight adult children, seven grandchildren and 2 great grandchildren. To my life "full of quiet desperation", thank you Henry David Thoreau. To my Bridges of Madison County bleak existence. To decades of loneliness that was once alleviated by Berry's Scrabble games and texts. To life without Berry and without hope of a future at age 80 with him, assuming his wife had departed by then.

That had been my secret plan. To spend the next 18 years getting to know Berry. Or whatever time Berry's wife remained on earth. When she went to her heavenly home, Berry would be free to live out our days together. Maybe by then a few of my plumbing issues could be fixed.

You know, the incontinent issues. Don't even get me started on my hurling food habit. At any rate, surely by then Berry wouldn't be so dang handsome and perfect, and we could be imperfect together, forever.

You see, I never wanted Berry to lose his lovely Dublin, Georgia life. I just wanted to bring a bit more fun. He never complained or spoke at all about his wife or work, but a happy man doesn't text, send pictures of his handsome self as well as pictures of his magnificent manhood in its fullest form (you know what I'm saying). A contented husband doesn't write salacious, bodice ripping prose to an online stranger. I hoped he could have it all – his family and career and an ultra-discreet mainly cybersex girlfriend. One that he would occasionally meet up with on his business trips.

The answer is no. Berry will never have it all. He can't. Ever again. I can only hope his family doesn't feed him to the alligators on the home estate. I have a few more only hopes. I only hope his death and circumstances stay in Georgia. No one in Minnesota needs to know. Right?

I don't need men contacting me so they can die with a smile on their faces. I don't need the hotel chain installing defibrillators in all hotel rooms thanks to new legislation called the Heartbreak Hotel Hand Job Act. Discreet. Private. Berry died and I want to slither away from my involvement.

I am back to Minnesota. Back to work. Listen to my robot voice: work is good. Working is good. Everything is normal. You are home. Home is good.

I have clients to see. Being a therapist is my true calling. Jack and Diane are one of my favorite therapy couples. But then most of my clients are my favorites. They are all survivors of drama, resilient characters in the tragedies of life. I admire them and want to help if I can.

Therapy Session: Jack & Diane

Quick Recap:
Jack is 69 and Diane is 63. Both are retired and living on social security and modest pensions. They have been divorced for over 10 years but live together to share expenses. Neither of them date other people. They are both very unhappy but apparently are stuck waiting for some miracle to happen. This is our 6th session. Diane struggles with depression, anxiety, insomnia, and compulsive overeating.

Jack is trim and relatively healthy. Diane is "puffy and fluffy", her terms. They both look "road hard and put away wet", one of my favorite expressions from Tennessee Ernie Ford.

Session:
"He called me a bitch in front of my daughter and 5-year-old granddaughter. He said he didn't give a fuck." Diane spat this out at her partner Jack. Jack retorted without any remorse, "She made me. She deserved it."

I let a silence fill the room, waiting for either partner to try and make a repair. No one spoke. They both glared at me in their singular righteousness. I knew from John Gottman's principles that a key to the impact of such an ugly row is that someone step up and offer a repair.

Neither partner spoke. I broke the impasse after about five long, squirmy filled minutes. I asked, "Do either of you want to repair the damage of this encounter? If so, you have a full minute to offer each other something to start a repair.

I didn't expect a repair attempt or an apology from Jack. Early in our therapy sessions I had come to appreciate that he exhibited clear characteristics of Asperger's Syndrome, now classified as part of a broad category called Autism Spectrum Disorder (ASD) in The Diagnostic and Statistical Manual of Mental Disorders (DSM-5). Subsequently Jack, Diane and I had spent several sessions exploring behaviors, responses and forming realistic expectations of each other.

Jack was academically intelligent. He had a font of expertise across subjects from animal husbandry to the composition of a Ziploc baggie. He also had unmanaged anxiety which seemed to explode in rage, meltdowns, and angry withdrawals. As Diane called it, Jack "bolted" not just from a room but would pack and leave the room, the home, travelling across the country. He left wreckage, disbelief, fissured trust, and betrayal behind. None of which he could recognize before, during or afterwards.

No, Jack wouldn't see the connection between apologizing or offering any responsibility for his actions as a repair effort and the present hostility between he and Diane. Jack was unable to offer a repair. His assumed diagnosis is based on his impenetrable, imperviousness to other's emotions or perceptions. Jack as always remained noncommittal to change or the commitment to try and improve the relationship. At the onset of therapy Diane was worried that she had married a narcissist. She felt crazy because Jack caused her to feel so needy and unsatisfied emotionally. She saw him as so self-absorbed and unloving. But narcissism and someone with Asperger's Syndrome are quite different.

Jack was not a smooth operator, purposely manipulating Diane. Jack was socially awkward and frequently misunderstood conversations, jokes, and teasing. Jack's comments were perceived by others as quite rude, but they were absent malice. Jack felt he was being factual.

Diane was in an Asperger-Super Woman pairing. Jack was attracted initially to Diane's niceness. Diane is easy going and affectionate. As Asperger's deficits prevent men (men significantly outnumber women in this diagnosis) from understanding the world around them, the Super Woman, with super nurturing skills makes his life easier. Asperger's is considered a social-communication deficit. Diane oozes social skills and fills in all the gaps for Jack. Jack married Diane in confidence that she would help him belong and feel okay in a confusing world.

Diane has company in the Asperger-Super Woman Club. Dianes (women like Diane) love to help, fix, and manage. Many have experienced a parent or close relationship with a strong Asperger's component and a

Jack (men like Jack diagnosed with Asperger's) seem familiar and safe. Dianes may have been in a vulnerable place when they meet a Jack – recent divorce, been cheated on, experienced a death or sickness. A Jack's appeal is their intellect and loyal presence.

Without realizing that she has married someone with social-communication deficits, the first clue of trouble may come in the bedroom. Some Jacks do not enjoy sex due to their sensory issues and a low sex drive. Combine that with the inability to read their partner and understand their partner has unmet needs. Generally, sex is quite unsatisfactory for Dianes. Conversely, some men with Asperger's may be overly sensitive and be overwhelmed. They may experience Erectile Dysfunction. Viagra is not the cure as some Jacks do not want to be sexual with a partner. Period. No matter the why, sex is complicated and problematic for Jacks and their partners.

When first seen for therapy, Diane was depressed with low self-esteem. Nothing she did improved her relationship with Jack – trying to implement "The Five Love Languages", "Men are From Mars, Women are from Venus", women's magazine tips, sexy lingerie, using his mom's recipes – all for naught. They divorced but continued a friendship of sorts. Jack still needed Diane's help in navigating family and work and social difficulties. Diane struggles to nurture her own needs and interests and consistently inadequately provides for her own emotional needs.

As predicted, Diane spoke first. "Jack, we can be good friends and work like a team. But I can't have my years of serving you be attacked by your calling me a bitch." Jack responded, "What else do you call always mocking me and putting me down?". Frustrated, Diane said, "You have no sense of humor. I can't even tease you a little."

I intervened. It was time for Jack and Diane to develop a trigger list. Both needed to create a list of words, scenarios, and warning signs they individually have. This is their homework. We will review their lists at our next session.

Jack wants Diane to know everything she does that angers him. Diane has presented as indifferent to the information in our sessions. I suspect she has emotionally checked out – something I need to ask. The question is if it should be asked at this juncture? What is the therapeutic benefit of having her answer right now? Not much value I sense. Jack needs to gain awareness of his own triggers, warning signs, stress, and sensory overload symptoms. This task is independent of its impact on Diane. Jack needs the information.

Diane can create a list for Jack of concrete examples of her issues as homework. Diane is highly verbal and will probably enjoy the homework, just to be doing something. Diane also shows a desire to control issues and people so the list will be extensive, I imagine. What will be interesting to read will be the clues why despite her unhappiness with Jack, she is still with him. Does Diane have some foundational philosophy that any man is better than no man?

Regarding Diane's aura of indifference, Jack seems indifferent as well. Is this indifference a defense mechanism they both use? For Jack, reminders that his behavior is not normal and is destructive to relationships – personal, familial, and professional - are necessary. I wonder how Diane conveys this information to Jack. Is there a way Jack could hear it without becoming defensive? The goal is to help Jack. How? Jack's frustration at not understanding others need to be appreciated. The caveat is he needs education, feedback, and opportunities to improve.

Diane appears defeated. Jack is stony appearing with his arms crossed looking anywhere but at Diane and myself. As this is our 6th session, I am wondering what I am missing about these two. They seem so miserable, yet they come, pay their admission but don't enjoy the circus. What is keeping them together?

I get paid the big bucks to ask the hard questions, so I ventured. "You both work so hard to stay together despite the difficulties, I am wondering why?" There was a noticeable difference in the room – like a breeze coming off a lake on a hot day.

Diane and Jack looked at each other and smiled. SMILED. I waited, appreciating the simplicity of a smile.

"If you've met one person with Asperger's, you've met one person with Asperger's." Stephen Shore, Ed.D.

Are you interested in more information?

1. Repair: John Gottman, www.gottman.com
2. The Seven Principles for Making Marriage Work, John Gottman
3. Asperger's Syndrome: Asperger/Autism Network, aane.org
4. "Asperger's Syndrome – A Love Story", Sarah Hendrickx
   "Aspergers in Love", Maxine Aston

Conversation Starters

Years and hardships can dull a relationship. Thinking that you each know everything about your partner certainly sounds boring. The following is offered as conversation starters to deepen your emotional intimacy. Whether you make this is a list to read, or write a question on the mirror with lipstick, or walk and talk, or drive to do mundane chores, maybe they will spice up life. It is not a race to finish the list but rather a way to express interest in your partner. Hope you enjoy these.

I broke the questions into groups and activities during which you might want a conversation jump starter:

Dishes and Dishing
Bedtime Stories
Breakfast Blues
Commercial Break/Driving
Dining Out
Slow Saturdays
Silent Sundays

Dishes and Dishing

1. Can you guess what attracted me to you?
2. What attracted you to me?
3. What is the craziest thing you have ever done (or done this year)?

4. What is your favorite memory from a childhood trip?
5. If you could be a wall – whose wall. would you like to be? What would you like to overhear?
6. What makes a person dislikeable?
7. If you could banish one or two persons from your life to the moon, who would they be and why?

Bedtime Stories

1. What would be the greatest gift to receive?
2. When are you the most "you"?
3. What's the nicest compliment you've received?
4. What is your favorite memory of someone who isn't in your life anymore?
5. If money were no object, how would you decorate our house?
6. What do you like most about where we live?
7. What small pleasures do you enjoy the most?

Breakfast Blues

1. Chocolate chip, banana, or blueberry. Which type of pancake would you choose to eat for the rest of your life? Oh, yeah, chocolate chip gives you the ability of flight. Banana gives you the ability of super speed. Blueberry gives you the ability to read minds. Which power would you most want in your day-to-day life?
2. Pickles, tuna fish, or ghost peppers. You must add one of these on every dish for the rest of your life. Which one do you choose?
3. A group of aliens invade your home and say that they'll take you away unless you can provide them with the perfect meal consisting of two sides, an entrée, and a scrumptious dessert. What is the best meal you'd make for them? Would it save you?

4. What friend have you not thought about in a long time?
5. What scandal happened in your neighborhood or town when you were growing up?
6. If you could open a business, what type of business would you open?
7. What untrue thing did you believe for an incredibly long time?

Commercial Break/Driving

1. Is it better to trust people or not trust people? And why?
2. What animal are you most afraid of?
3. How well do you think you could handle prison?
4. Do you believe in good luck and bad luck? How about things that are lucky or unlucky?
5. If you had a million dollars to give to any charity, what type of charity would you give it to?
6. What makes you feel super fancy?
7. What do you take for granted?

Dining Out

1. What's the most ambitious thing you've attempted?
2. What's the biggest opportunity you've been given?
3. What's a question you wish people would ask more often?
4. What are you most sentimental about?
5. What question do you most want an answer to?
6. What do you look forward to most in a day?
7. What's the most rewarding thing in your daily routine?

Slow Saturdays

1. What expression of affection from me makes you feel more deeply loved or appreciated?
2. What about that makes you feel that way?
3. In what ways have you longed for me to love you more?
4. What do you think God likes about our relationship? What do you think He would like to be different?
5. What are three of my favorite things about you?
6. Have you seen God work this week in your life?
7. What is the craziest thing you have ever done?
8. If you could have three wishes, what would they be?

Silent Sundays

1. What is my favorite song and what do you think it means to me?
2. What makes you dislike a person?
3. What would the best version of you be like?
4. How do you like to be romanced?
5. What interest or activity would you like me to be more involved in with you?
6. What is the most significant change you would like to make in your life?
7. What is one thing you wish you could say to people but can't?

Chapter Two

My mom taught me how to play Scrabble. I love to play and when I learned that Word with Friends (WWF) was an online Scrabble game that I could play 24 hours a day, I was hooked. I played anyone who would play me. I went from being thrilled at achieving 20-point words to striving for 120-point words. I saw my average word play go from 16 to 28 points a play. Absolutely addictive.

Then I met Berry. Berry had been playing WWF for 3 years. His average word score was higher by an average of 50 points. He won me game after game until one day I won. He wrote in a chat box something like congrats. I responded something gracious like what a great challenge he was.

His WWF picture was attractive – movie star looks – salt and pepper facial hair and temples, a true Colonel Sanders Kentucky Fried Chicken's doppelganger! Yummy. I have a type – ever since age 5 or so. Berry was my type – dark hair, brown eyes, broad shoulders, tall, very masculine. After 50 + years I had barely evolved from my crush on Batman aka Adam West. Berry looked like an older, sophisticated Batman. Be still, my beating heart (quote from William Mountfort's Zelmane, 1705).

We evolved from pleasantries to sharing more. I began to check all day long for a message from him. If he wrote, I would glow inside and whatever hideously boring thing I was doing suddenly wasn't so bad. I could literally dance through the laundry of 11 adults and 2 grandchildren, their endless dishes and meal prep became less discouraging.

My anti-marriage militant stance was slightly softened. (Yep. I am an anti-marriage Marriage Therapist.) Suddenly my stance changed to "Oh, this is why people marry". They become in love with another person's good traits. As a therapist I seldom see this part. I only see the fallout from Hiroshima-type fights and Nagasaki size disagreements. It was tough not to be disillusioned. And that is before my own two forays into self-less, unrequited servitude enslavements…i.e., marriage #1 and #2. More on these uncivil wars later if we really have to rehash the nightmares.

Yes, Berry was a bridge to excitement, fun, the piece of my soul that was encased in scar tissue so thick to protect the layers of injury underneath. Add to this his complimentary nature and I became a swooning female under his charming flirtations. I will not oversell and under deliver. Here are some of the witty repartee's we shared.

Read these text messages please. Is the feeling of fun and romance mutual or have I been completely deluded? Do you detect a potential for love?

Berry: *Naughty girl. Let's say your word selection is provocative.*

Me: *A little ribald vocabulary never hurt anyone.*

Berry: *Spiced up my Sunday. "Moob" (a word I just played) –
Thanks, I do what I can to avoid that look.*

Me: *How are you doing, besides relishing your smack down win?*

Berry: *I have learned that celebrating a win too heartily can come back to haunt one! So, taking a tempered approach to celebration.*

Me: *Are you an even keeled person in general?*

Berry: *Are you psychoanalyzing me? Answer is yes.*

Me: *Nope. I don't analyze without a request. Do you need anything?*

Berry: *Nope, just pulling your chain.*

Me: *I like having my chain pulled.*

Berry: (Sent an emoji of a smiley face)

Was that not scintillating? Gosh, I still smile at the exchange. That is either how desperate I am or how wickedly we were emotionally connecting! Other text messages just massaged my faltering ego as I massaged his probably massive one:

Me: *You are most deserving of my best efforts oh Master of WWF.*

Berry: *You're so suave, so smooth!*

Me: *What a sweet thang to say.*

There were also pictures sent via Messenger and one of my favorites was a picture of Berry after gardening. He was shirtless, sweaty but smiling with teeth – teeth showing which means happy to me. I started teasing him about gardening naked which made him send laughing emojis. This joke became our private thing.

Me: *Happy Friday! Any weekend plans for naked gardening and skinny dipping?*

Berry: *I told you, the gardening is SHIRTLESS. LOL*

Me: *A girl can dream.*

Did you know that Scrabble words can be risqué? That is my specialty, and Berry never missed the lack of subtlety. What a genius he was. Spoken by a 13-year old's heart trapped in an old women's body.

Berry: *Your wordplay is naughty once more.*

Me: *Cuz I know you like it.*

The best days in this past year started at 5:30 Minnesota time, which was 6:30 am in Georgia.

Me: *89 points! How did you score that? Good Morning!*

Berry: *Wanted to make sure I had your attention.*

Me: *You got it for sure!*

Berry: *Playing with you is hard work*

Me: *But pleasurable, yes?*

Berry: *Moments but reaching them takes know how. To make matters worse, your game photo is absolutely angelic*

Me: *I like your know-how!*

Berry: *So, when you make a big play and I want to call you bad names. I feel guilty.*

Me: *Ditto…kids know you as Scrabble Berry because I get frustrated at times!*

Berry: *But then you take pleasure, too, right?* (rose emoji)

Me: *Don't get the big head, but it is the best part of my day.*

Berry: *No big head here and thanks. I enjoy it as well. Cuba Libre time?*

Is this man absolutely charming or what? Or because my comparison is to the vacuum cleaner which refuses to scoop up Legos and Barbie Doll hair, I just don't have any perspective?

Here is another thrilling text on what Berry liked on NETFLIX. Is this not a show of emotional intimacy?

Berry: *The Ranch is a favorite. Tudor's. Last Kingdom*

Me: *Thanks! I am happy to explore new shows.*

Side note – I had Sam Elliott's doppelganger for a client. Absolutely disarming. Plus, this client was extremely horny/charming, and he was 74. On our last session he kissed me with the speed of a cheetah…he was incorrigible. I think his depression had clearly resolved!

Berry: *That is a unique combination, horny, and charming. I'm sure you brought out the best in him, good looking therapist that you are.*

Deep sigh. Do you know that in 62 years, I had never, ever been told I was good looking? Neither husband. No boyfriends. No mom or dad. Yet when I turned 50 and had a Glamour Shot picture taken, they asked to hang a 20 x 24 copy in their shop for advertisement. Would a national chain want a picture of a hound dog, jowls, and all, with make-up on? Just to show their make-up artists can work magic? Wait…wait a minute. Was my picture showing that any haggard, heavy weight, horse-faced woman could be beautified…oh no. Another glimmer of positive self-esteem shattered. Thanks a lot.

If Berry did not have an attraction to me, there was the competitive component that added fun:

Me: *165 points? All time high!*

Berry: *happy to know you had a hand in helping me reach that climatic number*

Me: *Hate being helpful…*

Berry: *"Blypse", give me a break*

Me: *Mr. 165+ point word is schooling me?*

Berry: *No Doctor, Mr. 165 is beating you! Rack 'em!*

Me: *That was a close game. You are on my list now.*

Berry: *Close is not necessarily bad, raises excitement level. Think of it like that*

Me: *Being on my list is like being brushed by a butterfly…I'll be gentle.*

Berry: *Happy shall I be to occupy such a gifted position...*
Brushed by a butterfly

Fingers flying, we play a few more exchanges.

Berry: *Losing gives you a potty mouth I see.*

Me: *Oh, my apologies, I thought that was a Jewish term...*

Berry: *Old English, to the best of my knowledge. Ha-ha*

Me: *Vulgarity, oh dear.*

Berry: *At least I'm not really offended.*

Me: *Perhaps you have uttered a bit o profanity over the years?*
Episcopalian style?

Berry: *Alas. It is so. But never for higher score.*

Me: *Brutal blow*

Berry: *I tried to think of a tender way to say it*

Me: *Operative word "tender", you are forgiven.*

Berry: *Whew*

Me: *You are waaaaay too charming.*

Berry: *Thank you, perhaps a reflection of the WWF company I keep.*

As you can see there is a progression to our texts. You will never believe what happened a few days later! Read on:

Me: *133 points? What????*

Berry: *Good morning. To go along with your second cup of joe.*

Me: *No gallon of Diet Coke will massage this intellectual injury!*

Berry: *I know that steel trap brain of yours is already on the mend*
and looking for new ways to put you on top

Me: *So wickedly kind of you...good grief*

Berry: *You deserved that one*

Me: *Spank me good daddy...*

Berry: *ha-ha*

Berry: *Your play was surely venomous well played*

Me: *I had a choice of a benign word or venom... Want to keep things lively for you!*

Berry: *You have a talent for lively...I'll try to repay for favor in kind*

Me: *Your fine intellect requires it*

Me: *Speaking of someone needing a good spanking? "Nuddy"?*

Berry: *Blame it on your liveliness...Does something for me.*

Me: *Senor, there are many things I can do for you...like try to win more often!*

Berry: *I was on a different level. Don't overthink this move.*

Me: *What level were you on?*

Berry: *Well, the level I was not on was you winning more games*

Me: *Ah...perhaps you were in a bodice ripping state?*

Berry: *Yo're being naughty*

Me: *Bit of Episcopalian repression?*

Berry: *ha-ha. I'm human, struggle with that.*

Me: *I bet. I am truly being naughty and disrespectful. My apologies.*

Berry: *I'm playing with you. No need for apologies. Your naughtiness is always appreciated and welcomed.*

Me: *You totally got me dude. I just had ice cream in remorse. I felt so bad. Whew.*

Berry: *NO, no, no don't try to pin the ice cream on me. You're full of naughtiness this afternoon. You might need a spanking.*

Me: *True. On all accounts!*

Berry: *You're a lusty girl*

Me: *You have NO idea!*

Berry had NO idea that he was transforming this Petite Plus (gloried term for short fatty), Cherry Brown haired (thank you L'Oréal), freckled elder. The body under the face was scarred from multiple surgeries and had kankles big as tree stumps (for you skinny biotches reading, kankles are when there is so much leg fat the ankle disappears leaving a trunk attached to a foot). In your mind, conjure that I looked like Danny DeVito might if dressed in drag.

What was not transformed but just enhanced was Pepper, the person. Inside the unsightly body was someone capable of fierce love, loyalty, and passion. If you follow horoscopes, you will immediately recognize that as a Libra, I have a rich inner life. Berry was touching my inner life, from online, of course. True to being a Libra I was falling hard in like with Berry. I was bracing myself for falling hard in the next L word that follows "like". And pesky fleeting thoughts of eating my mate like a praying mantis, were barely kept in check.

My therapy practice benefitted from my renewed energy and optimism. I was transformed from thinking love didn't exist for anyone but children to understanding that love doesn't hurt. It's the one you choose to love that's hurting you.

Therapy Session: Ed & Eddie

Quick Recap:

Ed, the husband, is 42 years old. Eddie is the wife, is 45 years old.

They are both teachers with Masters' Degrees, fully tenured in their school districts. No kids although they both feel ready to parent. Both are athletic and enjoy running 5Ks for charity. They are a hard-working couple who do not flatter themselves with make-up, hair coloring, the latest trends in clothes. They come from divergent backgrounds as Ed was raised in a traditional Italian family and Eddie grew up in various homes, with and without her mother.

Session:

When I enter my therapy office, I wipe my feet on the welcome mat, leaving all my troubles outside the door. I am here for my clients and their issues. I try to stay focused through the sometimes tedious, repetitive fighting and delusional thinking, injecting a bit of logic or new perspective where I can. Ed and Eddie (not their real names, of course) are on their 5th marital counseling session. I admire their commitment to addressing the issues of their 24-year marriage. Not all the hurts, betrayals, and disappointment, can be fixed in a weekly 55-minute session. I am not a magician!

As I review their history and refamiliarize myself with where we left off and what homework was assigned on the last session, I am emerging from my cold war with my partner Bob, the frantic teeth brushing protestations of the 5- and 6-year-old grandchildren, the frustrated look from my daughter, the dog's idiotic barking at the neighbor's roofers, the sense of hauling my ever-present fat ass around yet another day. I start begging my mind to leave my stuff – all of it – so I can serve my clients. Troubles leave me alone, please.

Ed and Eddie push the door in with heightened angst and raised voices. Here we go Pepper. You can do this. I exchange pleasantries and read the body language. Quite a bit of tension. Someone has left the homework assignment at home, just as they are always leaving something behind, something undone, and it never has changed for the past 24 years. Sigh. Session in progress. Let us begin.

Ed and Eddie were assigned homework last week. Despite their screaming matches, the intensity of sound is not a predictor of marital distress. Fighting does not indicate the end of a marriage. There are techniques to fight fairer and arrive at some sense of mutual satisfaction. This was their homework – learning to actively listen and validate each other.

Think of the Olympics of Emotion in Marriage. Ed and Eddie were asked to use "I" statements when discussing an issue. They were to start with a micro small disagreement to practice on. I was hoping for an insignificant one such as shoes collecting in the entrance of their home. Easy, problem solving, not heavy with emotion. Did they go for an ant-size burden? Of course not.

Ed and Eddie proudly announced they discussed remodeling their kitchen versus using the funds for a trip to Europe. Wow. I inwardly braced myself for what surely would follow as the most soul crushing, mercenary discussion. I looked up expectantly searching their faces for clues. I sneak a glance at the clock hung just between their heads on the back wall. Forty-five minutes left. Let's do this.

Ed started with his side of the argument. Yep, no active listening done. Just brutal facts and dollar figures. Eddie interrupted with her desire to see Europe and leave the house in its demise as in a desperate run-away fantasy. We will review active listening again and practice. And then more practice at home.

But…the protests begin…it seems like we just go in circles. Ok, more instruction needed. I had Ed and Eddie arrange their chairs to face each other. Beginning with Ed sharing a childhood memory of his childhood kitchen, I gave him a few minutes to recall and briefly describe it.

Ed's childhood kitchen was decorated with red rooster wallpaper. His mom liked red, so his dad built a red booth for everyone to snuggle in and eat. The kids fought over sitting in the apex of the booth. The booth seats were red vinyl. His mom made red place mats with roosters embroidered on them. They ate most meals together as he was growing up. His dad was a postmaster and would walk a block to his work after breakfast. At lunch they all gathered to eat with their dad. After work, the dad was home at 4:45 sharp and they would have dinner and play ball in the front yard. His mom would save the dishes and clean up for later and sit on the front cement step, smoke glamorously and watch dad and the boys play catch.

For teaching active listening, I gave Eddie a sheet with questions to ask Ed. The questions would demonstrate interest in learning more. By asking follow-up questions, it would prove that emotionally she was curious about how Ed felt about the kitchen memory. This formal format of active listening teaches social interactions that foster rapport. Eddie was to learn information that helped her understand Ed better. Eddie was instructed to watch Ed's body changes as its own language and then to be aware of her body's own changes to the information. Lastly, Eddie was to grow in patience as she richly and deeply allowed Ed to explore this memory.

After Ed had described his favorite memory and Eddie had responded in all the ways an intimate listener can respond, I asked Ed how he felt. He was visibly relaxed, pleased and looked at Eddie like she was an angel of mercy. Eddie of course was proud of herself but frenzied for her turn.

After Eddie's example, Ed needed fewer prompts to respond to Eddie's favorite memory of her childhood kitchens. However, what the three of us did need was basically 3 tissue boxes because Eddie gave a most sorrowful description of empty cabinets, dirty dishes scattered on counters, chairs buried under yellowed newspapers, ants crawling into take-out food containers and a mom bleary-eyed, collapsed on a broken spring couch. Television in the background 24 hours a day. Overfilled and soggy grocery bags loaded with all manners of garbage, including kitty litter. Liquor bottles instead of milk cartons. Drinking out of cupped hands because there was nothing clean or that didn't have a splash of beer and cigarette ashes floating in it. Rough revelations.

Can you imagine how the happy, family filled kitchen Ed wanted to replicate was in such contrast to that of Eddie's childhood? Eddie came in for individual counseling so I hoped she would process whatever emotional reaction she had either now or at our individual sessions. I understood why travel to Europe wouldn't be far enough to leave those haunted childhood memories behind.

I concluded the session asking what Ed and Eddie wanted to do for homework. I was aware that we had opened a raw, festering sore. It was their choice to put a Band-Aid on it or treat it as the infectious wound it was in their marriage. They chose to do nothing. But they chose it together, holding each other's gaze and very nearly touching their fingertips to each other's.

As they opened the door to their new reality, I made my cryptic notes and rested. Rather than reflect on how good a therapist I am and how remarkably well this session went, I had a split second before my own problems came down the raceway, each one vying to be first to confound me and demand a response. I had turned my cell phone back on and it was buzzing itself as though to explode. Now what? Now who? How much? When is it needed? Which hospital?

Sigh. Deep sigh.

Any chance Berry texted? Berry, my drug of choice.

Are you interested in more information?

1. Active Listening – First named by Carl Rogers and Richard Farson in 1957!
2. There are lots of books for relationships as well as business soft skills development on how to become an active listener.
3. Here are some examples of active listening responses. Incorporating any of these will help make you a better listener and create understanding and appreciation of others.
    a. "Tell me what I can do to help."
    b. "How do you feel about ________?"
    c. "I'm sorry that happened to you."
    d. "Thank you. I appreciate your telling me this."
    e. "So, you are thinking ________"
    f. "I see you are upset. What's the worst thing or aspect of this for you?"
    g. Asking specific questions to gain a better understanding – not to be used to formulate an argument.
    h. "Tell me more about that…"
    i. Lastly – please use this carefully – you can disclose your own similar situation. Please only use this if it might help the other person. Do not use this for your own gain.

Conversation Starters

Pillow Talk Version

1. Would you like a star named after you?
   What would you like the star to be called?
2. If the only sex toy we could ever use was a box of Q-tips,
   what would you do with it?
3. What is the best part of sleeping together?
4. If one of your hands had to be attached for life to me,
   where would you want it placed?
5. What could I do to make sure your morning
   starts off in the best way?

Chapter Three

Some therapist I am. I am taking advice from the 75-year-old cashier at a Dollar Store. I was at the register when her manager asked her to work overtime because another employee hadn't shown for the shift. I said sadly to the elderly woman that I was the mother of one of those no-show type employees. We talked about why people do not show, don't call if they aren't coming to work. Eventually I blabbed that my 28-year-old daughter was acting like alcohol was her passion and mere activities such as living, working, volunteering, being a friend, daughter, doing her own laundry, cleaning her room – not even a passing interest.

The cashier's wrinkly eyes, all knowing, told me to give my daughter a drop-dead date to get her stuff together. I went to school for 25 years for a degree just to give my clients the same advice. One can't buy wisdom. Wisdom comes from butt kicking life events. Apparently, she had them in spades by the fact that she was still working a minimum wage job with a 24-year-old pimply boss. Had it not been for the line of bargain seekers behind me, I would have stayed to gleam her advice on other issues. I have plenty to choose from.

Among my purchases was a new Fall door hanging for my mom's memory care unit apartment door. God bless my mom. I tried to change the décor of her senior suite of the memory unit to match the seasons. Something new that she might notice and delight in, any mental stimulation hopefully helps. Although my mom has advanced Alzheimer's, she can still read most words. Not a lot of understanding, but an amazing ability to recite poetry from her days as a high school teacher. I visit nearly every day, so she recognizes me most of the time.

The plastic yellow and red flowers are in my cart, and not because I have horrible decorating taste. My 88-year-old dad, who insists on living in the huge family house that he cannot care for, wants them for the plastic planters on the front porch. The plastic flowers were a homage to how nicely his front porch used to look with the abundant Chrysanthemums that my mom maintained. I had purchased a quick toy to distract my 5-year-old granddaughter who begged for new Barbie dolls as rewards. My 6-year-old grandson got an equivalent gift to be fair. There were birthday cards for my stepson and his wife and for the next 14 birthdays falling in a single month. The efforts to meet the needs of two elderly parents, eight adult children, seven grandchildren and two great grandchildren and all their spouses and significant others consumed my non-working time, non-household slavery time.

In case you have already lost count, I am a custodial grandparent to my Littles, ages 5 and 6. I also have under my roof five adult children and their current love or sex-only interests and my partner Bob. There is a daily party of thirteen people (including me) occupying every square inch of my home. The appliances are the hardest working entities in the house – there are always two full loads of dishes waiting their turn for the dishwasher. The washer and dryer run nonstop all day – if I am home to run it. Otherwise, the laundry is a mountain of individual baskets stacked to the ceiling. My favorite recliner is buried under clean laundry that does not fold and sort itself – and how everyone gets their clean clothes back is somewhat of a mystery to twelve of the residents.

One of the garage stalls is dedicated to toilet paper and paper towel supplies, boxes of laundry detergent, dishwasher detergents, garbage bags, and the critical supply of Diet Coke (for me). The other two garage stalls contain the least used cars because the generous sized driveway can only park 5 cars and that leaves four cars rotating around the cul-de-sac. Turns are taken parking in the street as no one wants to be ticketed. The thought of parking on the grass is routinely raised but countered with, perhaps you are ready for your own place to live?

At my advanced age, my energy was depleted daily and very little outside my drug of choice, a Dairy Queen sundae, restored me. But I still could instantly flip my self-pity to gratefulness. I was blessed with family and kept grounded by their problems. But the greatest blessing was a text from Berry.

I sit in the parking lot and do a quick text check to see if Berry is active online. Yes!

Berry played the word "woody"! I respond:

Me: *GM, "woody"! Happy Friday!*

Berry: *Paints a certain image, heh? Happy "woody" Friday to you*

Me: *Are you planning a "woody" weekend?*

Berry: *Plans and execution do not always coincide. Are you?*

Me: *What plans would you like to execute this weekend?*

Berry: *Although we have never met face to face, I get the feeling you are adept at asking questions for which you know answers already.*

Me: *I hate to assume because people have such complex personalities and lives. You are a prime example of rich, fascinating depths.*

Berry: *Good qualities for a skilled therapist*

Me: *To which the response is, you would make a great one!*

Berry: *I'll probably do some lightly clad yardwork tomorrow.*

Me: *Yummy...lightly clad, you say?*

Berry: *Well, that was opposed to your reference to naked gardening. I can't write the word that means without clothes and rhymes with lewd. WWF is censoring my texts.*

Me: *Omgoodness! That is the least offensive word! Really? If censored, my mind would look like **********!*

Berry: *That's cause you have many exciting thoughts streaming through that organ, I take it.*

Me: *Only when you are online! Lightly clad gardener...*

Berry: *And you're never lightly clad up there in MN? You owe me a pic. Lightly clad, with a smile. Showing off your beautiful sparkling eyes.*

How I lived for at least one sentence from Berry. It was like a life saver thrown to a drowning woman who is dogpaddling for life in the Bermuda Triangle. Today felt like a cruise ship had come for me. Oh, thank you Berry. Thank you, God, for sending me Berry.

Therapy Session: Kramer

Quick Recap:

Kramer is 37 years old. He has been a policeman for 11 years. He shares custody of his two children, disharmoniously. He is clean, head freshly buzzed, well mannered. Clearly a sad countenance. Hasn't smiled once in a session. Does not respond to my making self-deprecating small talk to get him to soften up. Example: I apologized that my office once smelled like tuna. I wasn't thinking when I made my lunch. No response.

Session:

Kramer, a mid-career police officer whose days were spent patrolling scuzzy streets, always on alert for his own death or that of a doped druggie, came in for his weekly session. Kramer had started a new medication and was a referral from his psychiatrist. We were to meet weekly and monitor Kramer's depression. It was a privilege to work with Kramer's psychiatrist in collaboration. However, sharing the responsibility for such a critically depressed man was frankly, scary.

As it was, Kramer's sessions were an hour of me working too hard and him, not saying anything. Today I was planning to take a little poke at the bear. He had been on medications for depression, insomnia, and anxiety for almost a month. I had been respecting the silent, manly man, resistant attitude. Today I hoped he would respond. I was prepped to be of some help. Somehow, no matter what and despite Kramer's skilled attempts to thwart me, I would try.

Working with men – as a therapist, a partner, a friend – is problematic. Men generally lack emotional awareness, have an inability to express emotions and are limited in their ability to be intimate. (Caveat, being sexual is not the same as being intimate!). Men would protest this – after all they can express anger instantly! Yep, that's right. Anger is the only venue men can access with ease.

Of course, we can blame fathers for teaching the ease of accessing anger to their sons. However, educated, research- based society members disagree. The lofty experts state that mothers are to be blamed for not meeting the boy child's needs. However, they note the adult man is responsible for the rest of it. It is his life. Discerning anger, sadness, fear, shame, and guilt is essential for healthy relationships.

Kramer, when he does answer a question, is openly hostile towards his ex-wife, his parents, the scum of society, and having to waste an hour with me. I imagine that Kramer is mixing up his wants as needs, and his needs as wants. When confused by these, his anger grows.

His ex-wife wanted more Kramer and less cop when he was home. He tells me that he wanted more wife and less bitch. I suggested he needed more love from his wife, more connection and intimacy (beyond the bedroom). Nope, he thinks he needed more sex. Want versus need? He wanted more sex but needed more love, connection, and intimacy.

Today my plan is to be more of a coach and teach the skill of learning to vent. For the partner of a man – this means striving to not just let the guy be mad. It means when the man starts feeling something, we want to change our behavior. We want to teach our man that he can ask if he can just vent. Vent with NO advice desired, offered or given. He then talks and talks and releases energy and angst. When depleted, he can receive feedback like – I love you. I am sorry you are going through this. You can tell me more if you want. (Say nothing else, please.)

Today, I get to ask Kramer if he wants to just vent. No need to formulate an argument, become defensive, or even make sense. Just let it all out – good, bad, ugly, ugliest. I don't mention that maybe later we could process if venting reminded him of any childhood incident or memory and how he and his caretaker/parents/teachers handled it. We then could explore if something could be changed about this past situation, how would his life today be different. I tell you this in confidence. Don't practice this at your home!

Kramer is predictably uncomfortable. I throw the exercise out non-chalantly as just adding a tool in his toolbelt. He retorts that he has no one to vent to. I check to see if I am still in the room and smile at him patiently. Did I share that men have trouble receiving help? Yep.

Kramer plays the ambiguity dance – he is vague and not committed to the discussion. Ambiguity is like his armor. He won't let me in – there is so much fear. Fear of therapy, me as a woman, fear of having our therapy cliff notes available to his boss – there are some real, many perceived threats, a Titanic load of imagined threats.

So, we sit, and I resign myself to being present to his silence. Perhaps the next session will be the one in which he trusts me more, trusts himself, and gains a desire to move to a better existence.

Kramer yawns. The yawn means he is dissociating from therapy and his emotions.

Nick Wallace, MA, LMFT lectured on this at a Minnesota Family Therapy Convention and these words play continually in my mind, both personally and professionally.

Are you interested in more information?

1. Most men often have one emotion which is easily accessed and that is anger. Men benefit from therapists who understand the difference between anger, sadness, fear, shame, and guilt. The ManKind Project, USA has resources. Website: MKPUSA.org

Conversation Starters

Afternoon Delight

1. If no one were around, would you, skinny dip with me? Why or why not?
2. At what age should a child not see their parent(s) naked?
3. If you had a magic wand for just 5 minutes, what would you do?
4. If a video were made of your favorite time of day – what would the film capture?
5. If you had access to all the foods in the world, what would you like on a 2:00 tea tray or at a 2:00 snack?

Chapter Four

Do you know what a woodworking vise is? It's like two clamps that hold something in the middle while carpentry work is being performed on it, or while glue is drying something together. My life is in the middle of two industrial strength clamps.

One clamp is my family putting pressure on me. The other clamp coming from the other side is work and bills. I am in the center. Rather than becoming glued together, I feel like I am becoming unglued.

I keep a mantra that diamonds are made under pressure. Therefore, someday I will be a Star Africa, one of the largest and most famous diamonds in the world. But for today I am a lump of molten rock. And my Partner Bob is steel slag.

Do not get me started on Partner Bob. We are the oddest non-couple, and most of the time, non-friends. Our teamwork abilities are worse than China and North Korea trying to share nuclear weapons, identical twins fighting who is more attractive, two hungry grizzly bears on a fresh catch. So why are we living together? I don't know. I am tired of trying to figure it out. No more questions please. It is what it is.

Am I sounding rather negative? Why. Yes. I. Am. It has been over 29 hours since I have heard from Berry. He has not responded to any sparkling conversation starters I have provided. I am sad.

Sad turns mad. Mad turns to Google. (I am already three Dairy Queens into problem solving and need a new approach.) I type in "why won't married man respond to me?". And suddenly I am learning new things. Learning always helps me grow in understanding. Got something new to share: Breadcrumbing.

Holy Mother of Oprah! Yes indeed, this term matches what I am experiencing. Let me explain it and see if you find it helpful too. Breadcrumbing, according to the Urban Dictionary, is when your fantasy person, crush, date, etc.... has no intention of taking things further but they like your attention – but only when they want it, on their timing, on their terms. They have no regard for you except what you can do when they need something.

This isn't ghosting. Ghosting is almost a favor to you. If you are smart or are in therapy, you move on fast. Being breadcrumbed is painful. Breadcrumbers are leading you on because they don't know when they could use an ego boost from you. Oh great.

There are some significant signs Berry is breadcrumbing me. I am such a doofus – Berry sends a "hey PJ". I am thrilled he has texted my initials! What is WRONG with me? It is a lazy man's text. Desperado me. Why do I equate my initials as akin to roses and chocolates being delivered to my room with a singing telegram? Good grief. I am needier than I thought.

A second clue to see if you are being breadcrumbed: is the relationship moving forward? If a person is into you, they will want to increase their time with you. Like I knew this. Duh. I have only watched the movie "He's Not That Into You" like fifty times. I read the book. I keep re-reading the book. My favorite lines are pink highlighted, and tear stained. Like a fountain of wisdom, sarcastically delivered: "Assume you are the rule, not the exception."

"I know it's an infuriating concept – that men like to chase, and you have to let us chase you." (Being a Ph.D. doesn't exclude me from chasing Berry. Must slow my roll. Be cool Dr. Pepper. Chill.)

Third, there are no excuses. No text message is saying something. It says it all. No one who wants to be in "like" with you will let anything, but death, separate them from their cell phone and contacting you.

Fourth is your choice – stop responding to the dribbles or ask your "elephant in the room question". The dribbles of sporadic text messaging should be a big enough clue. But if you need to have a concrete response, ask your question. Then give them a truly short response time – like 48 hours. And then move on.

If you receive no response, you've been breadcrumbed. You will survive. That is why Dairy Queen is an international franchise with plans to build on the moon. Where people are, there is misery, thus purchasers of Peanut Buster Parfaits.

There are other signs of breadcrumbing, but they all translate to the breadcrumber doesn't want to get to know you. They stay on a superficial level; they cause you worry and then roller coaster you to happiness with a short text. Maybe you have become their booty call or cybersex "mon ami".

Please note: Mon ami is not French, Italian, or Spanish for love interest. It means buddy or friend. How international and suave of them to use this term. How dumb of us if we are tickled and tantalized by it.

Therapy Session: Jerry & Janice

Quick Recap:

Jerry and Janice are both 55 years old, pruned, and groomed. The have been married 40 years, having met in high school. They are seemingly alcoholics and deny using other substances. But they also deny being alcoholics, so who knows the truth?

Session:

Jerry and Janice arrive for their 11th marital therapy session in the throes of alcohol fueled arguing. I can smell booze and cigarettes emanating from their skin. I recoil in my seat. Today's session will be perhaps their only hour without a drink today. And for this couple, that alone makes for a valuable and billable session.

The rule is to cancel the session if the person(s) arrive inebriated, high, or stoned. One cannot focus on change in this soggy, spacey mental state. However, this couple rarely is sober for me. Moreover, once I even called the police when they left. I felt compelled to report they were driving under impaired conditions. It didn't slow their imbibing. And they scheduled with me again, even though I am confident they knew it was me who called the police.

With a longing gaze at the clock, I began the session. Janice had lots to say. Her handsome husband was in deep trouble with her. She had frequently complained about his online gaming habits. This week she had uncovered his messages to a fellow online Bridge player. She had taken great pleasure in printing them out for me to read.

I read a bit to satisfy Janice but my opinion of what the messages were about was not important. The issue was what did the messages mean to Jerry and what did they represent to Janice. Even though it may be obvious to you and me that messages outside the marriage to another woman can be bad news, I have to ask questions and not just assume I know what Janice objects to. I had to suspend my own anxiety over being in an online relationship with a married man. I mentally put my anxiety on the outside of the office and locked the door, so I could focus on the couple's process.

Janice had some familiar sounding responses – Jerry was flirting, he was having an affair, he was taking time from his marriage to become involved with someone else.

When it was Jerry's time, he talked about the innocence of having a friend. This new friend lived 3800 miles away and was married too. It was mostly just an incredibly competitive Bridge game.

I waited patiently. After protesting the innocence of something usually the next step is to retaliate back with the shortcomings of the spouse and how they almost drive a person to cheat. The spouse ignores them, is cold and unloving, doesn't seem to care, blah, blah, blah. The justification is the 3rd step, so I steadied myself.

Yep, having an online friend is so safe Janice should appreciate how Jerry is protecting the marriage by using this little vehicle to get some of his needs met. Sigh.

The session time is over. How can I end it after this implosion? A therapist never has to have any answers. Cool job, really. What we need is to ask the couple what answers they can generate to resolve their issues. So, I asked J and J what they wanted to do about this.

Somewhat sober after almost an hour of detox, they volunteered to talk more in the upcoming week. I asked that they bring a list of 10 things they came up with to solve the issue. They looked at me with blank, blurry eyes and stumbled out of the room.

As you read this account and form your judgement as to my efficacy as a therapist, be gentle. Jerry and Janice have refused rehabilitation and treatment options. Those discussions happened early on in our therapeutic relationship. I am resigned to monitoring their level of angst towards each other and the drama of their favorite bar. I have performed community service by encouraging public transportation to my office and notifying police when they leave my office. Not sure what they would do to each other if they didn't have their weekly referee sessions.

I know what I would do with their hour, should they not reschedule! I effectively gain 90 minutes because their hour causes such a smell that I spend the next 30 minutes disinfecting and deodorizing my office so the next clients don't think I am the alcoholic. I could be scheduling someone who respects our sessions, does their assigned homework, experiences exponentially wonderful personal growth, pays in cash, attributes their much-improved mental health to me, and who actively nominates me for recognition or sainthood.

Are you interested in more information?

1. Harm Reduction: it is a proactive stance to reducing the damage suffered by addictions to alcohol, drugs, gambling, sexual behaviors.
   Harm Reduction does not try to "save" through rehabilitation, it just supports a client wherever they are. It encourages the client to take responsibility for their health and safety and offers support with the belief that it is possible to control the addiction and live a productive life.

2. ENRICH – This is the married couple's enrichment program. The official title is PREPARE-ENRICH Program.
   To find a workshop or a facilitator:
   www.prepare-enrich.com or search for PREPARE-ENRICH Group Programs or online programs. The foundation of PREPARE-ENRICH is based on Systems Theory, Couple and Family Strengths Model and Prevention-oriented approaches.

Conversation Starters

Happy Hour

1. If you could change one thing about today, what would it be?
2. How would you like to be introduced to a gathering of 100 strangers?
3. What political promise would you make and try your best to keep?
4. If you could start your own town on the moon, what would you name it and what would be the town motto or slogan?
5. If you had to return to earth after death to either fly or swim, what animal would you choose to be and why?

Chapter Five

Berry became more interested in me. I was flattered. At last, someone who was more my equal intellectually, spiritually, and emotionally! I presumed we had around the same incomes, were two years apart in age, both quite religious, family oriented, and breadwinners for our households. Berry's degree was in Communication. My job was all about talking and improving communication. Berry was employed as a Grand Puba, ala Fred Flintstone, for a national widget manufacturer. (Apparently, he could play Scrabble during conference calls without missing the urgency and importance of the all-important business at hand.)

We both liked to write. What began as silly bodice ripping teasing texts eventually became cybersex with Berry experiencing a lot of enjoyment if you get my intimations. And when Berry's python came fully alive, he would send me pictures. Pictures of his python. Yep.

For my younger readers. Yes, a 64-year-old man's ramrod can be the most beautiful sight. Yes, 64-year-old men can still have sex. So can 62-year-old women. Life doesn't end at 30, 40, 50. In our 60's we may be the most sexually active! And randy? Yes. Raunchy – yes. We grew up with sexual freedoms exploding all around us. We may have done things you haven't even heard of - yet. So, don't go looking at your parents as walking corpses. We knew fun and still want it. Plenty of it.

Berry's is my first dick pic ever received. I am shocked. Bit scared. Impressed – nice and straight – no Pyrone's curvature on this guy! Pretty hefty girth and length to match Berry's 76 inches of height. Oh my. No wonder Berry keeps saying he has been blessed. Dang. Your jock cup runneth over.

I Google slang words for penis. You will find over 150 words. It seems I always divert being uncomfortable and try to intellectualize a situation. But this first picture dismantled everything I thought I knew. Googling was the only thing I could do to try and understand.

It was not like I had anyone to talk with about this. Good God, no. Absolutely no one who knew me as stuck in my 1970's hairdo, wearing my skirts hitched up like when I was 16, wearing a Walmart pearl necklace to wash the kitchen floor, struggling to get off a chair with my arthritis, would believe anyone could be interested in me. I was seen by my family and friends as an aging Norma Desmond character whose best days were behind her.

My Myers Briggs identifies me as INFJ – Introverted, Intuitive, Feeling, Judging.

I have the still waters run deeper than an ocean Myers Briggs rating. Literally there is no one who gets me. I am complicated per my INFJ description but can handle complexity.

A dick pic, however, is out of my wheelhouse entirely. I am trying to be logical and stay intellectual, that's Logical Pepper. I am so multi-faceted I can't even count my sides. There is another side, side two of Pepper James, love goddess. Side three is Pepper James googling websites that make wallpaper out of our photos. I want me some wallpaper of this magnificent dick picture. Customized Images will make one for $574.00. Side four of Pepper James is 13-years old and very giggly.

Looking at my Google searches would reveal more about my facets than anyone could imagine. From how to get a child's pee out of upholstery, how to move an egg laying turtle off my lawn, to resources for a mother whose child died by playing with noncustodial parent's gun, to the thesaurus word for "wet", calories in egg salad sandwiches, cost of a Dairy Queen franchise (I need to support my habit), cheap summer dresses for petite plus sizes, images of what women are supposed to look like at 62, recipes for making my dad food that avoids his allergens…, how to get a criminal charge against LC – a violent spouse, why married men cheat, is cybersex morally wrong and where in Georgia does Berry live. The theme is I like to understand things.

Here is something that I do not understand. I am not sure how breadcrumbing works with dick pics, but I surely was confused. And incredibly attracted to more than his mind.

True confessions time. After 16 years of being celibate (no man) and 40 years without an orgasm, I found my 1978, $9.99 vibrator. Bit o rust, bit of a funky love canal smell, but in working condition. More emotions came flooding out – I was buzzing in orgasms, confusion, and attraction, now add guilt, shame, shock, cha-cha giddiness, a sensation of the ghost of Pepper past coming back.

And amidst my titillating tinging, there was the buzz of my cell phone. It wasn't Berry, sad sigh. I opened my email to Our Family Wizard to read the latest diatribe from Larry Cockermouth (my daughter's violent ex spouse). LC – is my ex-son-in-law. He is the criminal brute who assaulted my beautiful daughter to an unrecognizable state and walks around free. Yes, his parental rights are severely limited, and the kids are safe in my custody. But nothing short of an execution will ever be fair and just. My faith in a heaven and hell bring me such comfort when I see injustices on earth. Thank you, God, for hell. Got someone to keep the devil company for an eternity. I cannot recommend him enough.

LC is illiterate. We are court ordered to communicate through Our Family Wizard, so that the tone of our writing is monitored, and social workers can review. Not sure the judge understood how academically impaired LC is. I raised 8 kids who learned to read and write and yet I cannot recognize his words as even the imaginative spelling of a first grader.

What is clear is that daily for the past 5 years, LC has launched venom at me. What is it today? Some days he launches repeated missiles of hatred. What will today bring? LC's vitriol becomes an ear worm. Think of a toddler hearing that they are going to be a big brother or sister. They clap their hands over their ears and start making a buzzing noise.

I am buzzing.

No matter what Larry Cockermouth tries, the beautiful children, made by his two sperm that were of roughly 50 micrometers each, are mine. The judge certainly saw through Larry's protests about being a loving father who only wants to bring his kids up right, albeit that means manhandling them physically to teach them "thar" manners. The judge also saw through Larry's attempt to burn my beautiful home of 30 years down. Although Larry was unsuccessful at burning his own children up in the fire that he set, and the police bungled the evidence, the judge still gave Larry a financial punishment for making me go to court again about him. So yeah. Larry, through the miracle of 50 micrometers, is attached to my back forever.

The cell phone buzzes again, and it is my savior on earth. Berry. Thank you, God. God who has given me just about too much to care for, rescues me. I give thanks for an illegitimate relationship. Oh well.

Berry: *You are playing like you're multitasking*

Me: *Oh my. Am I playing like a distracted moron???*
(I then played the word "cock".)

Berry: *Not at all. In fact, your word selection made me smile*
I'm surprised the censors let it go by

(Berry adds a "y".)

Me: *Bit "cocky" are you?*

Berry: *You supplied the root word my dear*

Me: *You augment quite naughtily.*

Berry: *You bring it out.*

Me: *If it's out…take a pic?*

Berry: *Yes, it's out. You want to see a pic?*

Me: *I don't, if asking is offensive.*

We switched to Messenger. Nothing happened that didn't please Satan. I am watching a married man resurrect my dead soul. I am so naughty. Good grief Pepper, pull yourself together and put your tongue back into your mouth.

Therapy Session: Dan & Darlene

Quick Recap:

Dan, age 61 and Darlene, age 62. Dan is one of the top 100 highest-paid bio-pharma CEO's (I googled him.). Darlene is his supportive spouse. Married 33 years. To each other. Very handsome couple, scary rich and powerful.

Good morning to me. Dan and Darlene are on the schedule today. Roughest hour of my week. Here is why I earn the big bucks. This couple brings me to thoughts of early retirement. Before I see them, I pray to my loving, merciful God for peace and strength.

I also read John Gottman's works for solace. The Gottman Institute has years of research into marital distress and from this they can predict the potential for a divorce with 91% accuracy. Dan and Darlene could surely be headed towards divorce. But you be the judge.

Upon entering, the uber wealthy couple brush off invisible crumbs and lint from my couch in the most exaggerated arrogant way, I grimace inwardly and smile with big horse teeth outwardly. Sorry for the unseemly condition of the newish furniture. Sorry for the fresh linen smell that competes with Darlene's saturated scent of Chanel Grand Extract. Sorry I cannot flaunt wealth. I only charge you $250 an hour and most of that goes to my own therapist, a required expenditure after seeing you both.

Today's adventure in the playland of the grandiose, superlatively wealthy begins with the same arguments as the modest and poor couples face. Not!

Dan has purchased a mountain cabin – slash – mansion in Aspen, Colorado. It is a huge surprise to Darlene. She has vowed to never step foot in it. She wants it sold immediately.

I want to stop here and explain that if this couple were of modest means, we can look at the act as one of buying something and surprising the partner. I bought a $40.00 Foosball Table at a church auction as a surprise for my partner. Perhaps you have purchased as a surprise, a side of cow meat, or a used crock pot from a garage sale and are looking forward to the pleasure of surprising your mate. The pleasure doesn't happen. See how similar the problems of the rich and poor are?

The basic issue in Dan and Darlene's argument is that the surprise is unwanted. What can Dan do at this juncture? Dan has choices. But Dan being Dan resorts to Gottman's four Horseman approaches.

Dan has mad skills in criticizing, showing contempt, acting defensively and in stonewalling. Interested in hearing what these look and sound like? Hang on Dan is just ramping up.

Dan looks at me and shouts, "Darlene never wants to do anything I think is fun. She never listens to my ideas or gives me credit for knowing what a good deal is. This place is cheap compared to how fast the equity will increase. Just down the street is 301 Lake Avenue which costs $28.7 million. Using the house for a few years and letting the equity grow will make us a fast couple of million." Thus, the criticism is of Darlene's apparent financial short sightedness and her inability to be fun.

The garage sale crock pot was such a steal and will save money because it will cook all day and be ready at night. No more fast food. Your fast-food habit is so wasteful. You need to save money on food. Just hot crock pot meals every night. Surprise!

I had to buy the side of cow. My parents bought the other side and needed a partner. If you could cook at all, you would realize what a great thing this is. I am tired of frozen packaged meals barely heated. You need to learn to cook a good piece of meat.

This is criticism. Not a healthy response to issues. Not a winning method of keeping a marriage vibrant. Criticism is a predictor of marital distress and added to other factors, an indicator of eventual divorce.

Dan hops on the back of the second horseman – contempt. He is explaining in a very obnoxious tone that he doesn't know why he bothers to try to do something nice for Darlene. He really is too busy to have to explain his financial acumen to her. Not one breath he breathes in the effort is worth it for Darlene. Ouch.

Can you hear your partner spit, life is too short to be with you? Life is too hard to keep trying because you are this and that? If you hear this, think of contempt. It is a supremely hurtful horseman.

Dan isn't done with circling the bonfire of their marriage. He moves on to adding to the flames – defensiveness. He apparently can't do anything right by Darlene. He is always in the "dungeon". (The "dungeon" probably looks like a presidential suite at the Trump Towers. Oops, did I just demean Dan's heartfelt emotions? Sorry.)

Maybe you can relate. Maybe your partner in life just responds to you defensively. When asked if they are attracted to a co-worker, they retort, Of course I am not. Or another example, you ask, "Are you going out for a beer after work again?" "Yeah, but I didn't go last night, so don't make a big deal about it." Mmm...

Defending themselves. Is there any other way of dealing with an issue? Can you see that this approach won't solve anything?

Dan has circled his camp on the last horseman's back – stonewalling. Dan's stonewalling sounds like this. Nothing. The sound of silence. Or the clock ticking. Or a plane flying overhead. Or of your heart hardening. You are being ignored. You aren't worth your partner's effort.

In Dan's case he is done. Done trying. Done being married. Done with Darlene.

I have let Dan vent. I have let Dan show who he is. All Dan's words are just words. What do I mean by this?

Let's take a slight tangent. I once was in an office of a domestic violence shelter. On the wall was the best quote ever:

"They will show you who they are. Believe them".

Let that sink slowly in. Words spoken by an abuser - I wouldn't have hit you if you had just done... You always get me so mad... The kid should have stopped crying...Why do I have to always be the bad guy here? Don't you know you gotta do ________ fill in the blank?

They – people, partners, co-workers, bosses, ministers, waiters, etcetera – will show you. Show you – in actions. Their words are nothing. You can see their actions. Their actions show you who they are. If they beat the family cat, you, your child – they are beaters. If your boss says a promotion is soon but someone else is elevated – believe their actions. You are not getting promoted. The promise of a promotion is not an action. Your boss makes false promises. They are false.

Believe them. Believe their actions are who they are. Dan's actions tell who he is. He is a husband in name only. He is not acting like a husband.

Darlene sits through the galloping horsemen. She has been burned in the bonfires before. She knows she is outside the circled camp. She knows she has tried but cannot enter and cannot save the marriage.

But she stays. This marriage is about money as much as some original vows. Darlene gets a bit of comfort from the resources I recommend. And for 60 minutes she is in the room with her spouse. It may be like a date in hell but at least it's a date.

When it is my turn to speak, I recommend John Gottman's "The Seven Principles for Making Marriage Work". Darlene will probably read it. Dan will have his work minion maybe read it. Both minion and Darlene will gain lots of insight.

Maybe someday both will leave Dan. After all, Dan has already mentally and spiritually left Darlene. And the minion will most likely not be promoted…

Are you interested in more information?

1. The 4 Horseman of the Apocalypse are named after the powers of War, Famine, Pestilence and Death. Death is the only one mentioned in the Bible.

2. John Gottman identifies the 4 Horsemen and provides the Antidotes. You can find a quick overview at: www.gottman.com/blog/the-four-horsemen-the-antidotes/

Conversation Starters

After Dinner Cocktail Conversations

1. Your guardian angel blushed today, what did you say or do?
2. What did you do to make the world a kinder, more loving, happier place today?
3. How would you like me to romance you?
4. If you carved 15 minutes into tomorrow's schedule, who would you reach out to and why?
5. What was your favorite childhood game and what would an adult version look like?

Chapter Six

I am a long believer in Mary Poppins' "spoonful of sugar" philosophy. I have elevated the spoonful of sugar to pounds of sugar that make life's difficulties bearable. Like most Americans, I easily consume 180 pounds of sugar a year. But in the decade Mary Poppins fictionally lived, people ate just 90 pounds of the sweet stuff. I think it is because our lives are harder these days. Do you agree? Say yes, that there is some logic to this theory.

Besides having perhaps partially faulty logic, who am I? I am a mediocre marriage and family therapist. A little less inept as a mother. A bit even more capable as a daughter who loves her mom with Alzheimer's. An excited, loving grandmother to my three grandchildren. Through the confusion of step-parenting, I have more grandchildren and even two great grandchildren that I would love to get to know, separated by distance and life's busyness.

I am my elderly father's vote to live with, out of my 4 siblings should that time come. And just that lucky in most of my endeavors. (Mixed blessing – that will make 4 generations under one roof!)

At age 62 I have had gained some wisdom. It has been butt-kicked into me. If anything resonates with you, I am glad. If you have an issue with me, write your own book. This is my book and I have been writing it in my mind for 52 years.

By the way today the clothes dryer decided it was done with me. Partner Bob is on a tear about something inconsequential. (Whiskey and eggs for breakfast? Good choice. No Whiskey? Oh No!) My daughters are filled with angst over the things that happen when you grow up and refused earlier career counseling. My son has hit a new low on his credit score due to the logic of needing a newer, bigger, lifted truck to pull the 22-foot trailer he has not paid for yet, to pull the cars that he thought he could revive but remain mechanically gutted, and multiple open bank loans. Seems the difficulty of parking said menagerie of vehicles in a small apartment parking lot is more of a concern than all the money he owes…. The two grandkids I care for think I am a mean witch because I ask them to brush their teeth and put on clean clothes. I am waiting breathlessly for the next installment of why Larry Cockermouth despises me. Even the dishwasher is refusing to do its job and doesn't feel like washing the dishes as instructed to do so last night before I went to bed.

Every Wednesday I merge my personal and family schedule with my therapy practice's schedule. Throughout the week I add additional things onto the schedule and update the printed copy on Sundays. I distribute the family schedule to Bob and adult children that live with me. Then, I pray for strength to get through another week of children's school, extracurricular activities, doctor appointments, daily visits to my mom, grocery shortages, never ending shopping lists, home repairmen, endless beautification appointments to ward off aging and bill paying, dog care, social media maintenance, therapy clients, etc. Add daily homework and spelling and reading and volunteering and it is a crazed life. I am lucky I know. I have this level of busyness and family surrounding me with perpetual neediness…so great a feeling that I fantasize running away. Daily.

And in between everything – at stoplights, in parking lots, between clients, while watching my poor mom try to get food from the fork into her mouth, I sneak peeks at WWF for a text message.

Praise to the heavens! It is Berry and my day begins afresh.

Berry: *GMPJ* (Berry writes – Good morning Pepper James)
Who knew one can play contractions? I learn more every day.

Me: *What a wonderful trait – humble but an ever-evolving genius!*

(I insert a new word)

Berry: *What exactly does a TONGER do?*

Me: *Tongues long things*

Berry: *I imagine the lady friends of a TONGER smile a lot*

Me: *Or the male recipients*

Berry: *Good point*

Me: *Kinda rowdy this morning?*

Berry: *It's the words of yours*

Me: *Oh? As I am a near-nun innocent, whatever do you mean?*

Berry: *Now you're trying to make me feel bad for suspecting a near-nun of anything nefarious*

Me: *Hate to break it to you, but I think I passed nefarious, thanks to you, about 10 months ago! Imagination gone wild!*

Therapy Session: Amy

Quick Recap:

Amy is 52, appears quite muscular in her sleeveless blouse. She is dressed beautifully, make up highlighting her large blue eyes. She is a blond and wears her hair in a loose, youthful style.

Session:

Amy is an enthusiastic therapy patient. She nearly bubbles like a shaken cola when something becomes clear or fits into her puzzle. Amy brings in a bigness to therapy – loud voice, bold clothes, militantly political agenda, cussing that causes me to blush and her wild humor.

This is Amy:

"Fuck Dr. P"

"Oh, sorry I said fuck.

Fuck, I said it again.

Fuck I can't help it."

And away we go into the neverland of Amy and her pursuit of a man. This strong desire to be in a relationship with a man is the presenting issue. But people are so complex. What is not being said? Why hasn't this happened by her age of 50? Is this goal in Amy's best interests? Is there anything Amy might be doing to self-sabotage?

Amy is an amazing woman in many regards. She owns a large suburban home as well as a rental property. She has a master's degree in Health Administration/Health Care Compliance and earns more than I do. She raised a daughter by herself who is now an adult.

She is efficient in her home, uber-organized in all aspects of her work, has a very active social life and gets plenty of notice on Tinder, Zoosk, Plenty of Fish, etc.... She is a self-proclaimed expert at hookups.

"So what", you should be asking. What are we missing?

I have learned to listen. I have a foggy brain but a work ethic that still insists on perfect retention, so I take lots of notes as Amy talks. Here are some things that I hear:

"My supervisor asked me how much longer till I put my notice in to leave her department. That made me so mad. Wanna hear something funny? I put a spoonful of pepper into her coffee." Second example, "I expected if I gave him a blow job, the least he could do was get it back up and finish me". Third, "I tried to be Grace Kelly like you told me to, so I left the dealership but accidentally scratched the showroom car with my purse on the way out. They came screaming over to me and I told them to fuck themselves, if they can still find it."

I can help Amy in tiny ways. Miniscule ways for the most part. Amy is a gifted, talented, intelligent woman with characteristics of being a grandiose-type narcissist. I do not believe this is genetic loading or a personal character flaw. She had a horrific childhood and I have often told her to write her story as a tool to help her see where she survived, but at what costs. Amy's narcissistic behaviors are probably masking a deep sense of insecurity. Amy craves positive attention and recognition for her many, many strengths.

The desire for a man is overshadowed by a craving for sex. Sex is a form of attention that Amy constantly seeks. As if being a superior lover will guarantee that she will be loved. Constantly seeking ways to get love and affirmations, she is exhausted.

Hearing her daily schedule fatigues, but she loves to recite it because it garners admiration and verbal stroking. Amy gets up at 3:30 am to go to work out from 4 to 5:30 am on any equipment which would stagger the average person, particularly the average man. She comes home and walks her dog for an hour and chats up all the early morning neighbors. She grooms herself and is on her computer working by 7:30 am. She walks the dog again for an hour at lunch and hits the gym by 4:30 pm for a few extreme body-shaping classes. She walks the dog for another hour and then begins her first bottle of Malbec with a Keto dinner. She loves to entertain and often has guests and more Malbec until it is time for more gruesome workouts the next morning.

I genuinely feel positive regard for Amy. I sit here all mashed potatoes, mayonnaise and pounds of butter and acknowledge her tremendous self-discipline.

After she has divulged her week's efforts at finding a "real" man, I start talking about female role models. As mentioned, she likes the Grace Kelly example. What I am trying to help Amy create is a tool belt of role models she can draw from when she wants to provide "retribution" for any perceived slight. Mother Teresa, Oprah, Audrey Hepburn, Maya Angelou, and Doris Day are examples of altruism, intelligence, and leading by kindness.

We have worked together for several years and have almost achieved a 48-hour window in which Amy will not email or text the most aggravating, angry, unbalanced, inappropriate two plus page reply to someone. Amy has a quick mind and her impulsive retaliations come without mercy. The goal is to write the wraith but hold it. Read it over when she is calmer. Email it to me for reading. Do some other stress-reducing activity with her energy and angst. This has been enormously difficult as Amy's triggers are deeply rooted. It is not hard to find a baby root, accidentally hit it, and find it is attached to a root entangled in the earth's hot, iron core.

I assume you are gaining a sense of the hostility that Amy displays in relationships and interactions. She can become verbally abusive and has occasionally been physically abusive. Amy holds a lot of stress – her desire to be physically perfect, perfect in her job, perfect as a homeowner, a perfect friend, a perfect volunteer, a perfect dog owner – is overwhelming. Amy likes to think she has it all together, and I bet she does, eighty percent of the time. The remaining 20 percent is what starts the negative feelings, cues the cruelty, stokes the rage, and implodes over people, particularly male partners.

You may know someone like Amy. Knowing from a distance. Where it is safe. You may have learned that Amy's negative feelings are lessened by another person's pain. She is most likely not going to show empathy and can dish out some brutal reprimands and invalidate the feelings of others.

You note that it is not enjoyable, and highly painful to be on the receiving end of Amy's roller coaster speeding from love to hate. She may be your best friend on Monday, and you are soaking in compliments about your appearance, your intelligence, your work style, etc... but by Wednesday you are looking for shelter. By then she may have infiltrated your friend group or marriage and created fissures just for fun. "I was just fucking with your husband. Why is he such a prick about it?" And if you are out of the relationship with Amy, you can consider yourself entirely dumped. Do not go back for the swim towel, CD, wedding ring or whatever you left at her house. It may not be worth it.

Amy loves competition so fitness challenges and work quota challenges are very stimulating to her. She is one of the hardest workers I know, and she will win. If she can use you to win, it will be done, and not necessarily malice free.

Amy enjoys gossip as a sport so you may hear about yourself in an entirely new form. Be careful. Do not indulge your own gossip fetishes in the initial glow of the relationship. Try to divert the conversation. Be a Grace Kelly yourself.

Amy's narcissistic behavior can be seen in her emphasis on appearances and the acquisition of material items. She needs these to stay secure and safe. Hold on to your Walmart $9.99 purse and just admire her FENDI.

Amy is surprisingly receptive in therapy. I offer her unconditional positive regard and she is able to hear what I say. She allows me to give a bit of a different perspective and then is willing to "kick the tire" by taking it for a test run. If I had a magic wand, I would give baby Amy and child Amy, parents who were mentally and physically healthy and stand back and watch all the potential she has come to fruition.

Are you interested in more information?

1. Narcissistic Personality Therapists – www.psychologytoday.com provides a directory by location. Be sure to vet the therapist before your appointment to be sure they are skilled in this area.

2. Is there a cure for narcissism? No, however therapy can help. The goal is to build up the person's poor self-esteem, manage their stress and anxiety and help them have more realistic expectations of others.

Conversation Starters

On route to visiting the in-laws/ out-laws/cousin's motorcycle gang)

1. What are your best hopes for today?
2. What would be the worst thing that could happen?
3. Wouldn't it be fun if _______ happened? Fill in the blank.
4. If our car broke down, would you consider not fixing it and just making out for a while? Or something else?
5. Tell me about a time when someone did something that was a dealbreaker for you?

Chapter Seven

I walk robotically to my gruesome grey 8 passenger mom mobile. Another day, another dollar earned. Pervasive loneliness fills my hollow core. I have given it all to my work.

I check my text messages, my social media, my Scrabble games for any friendly greetings...anyone, anywhere that wanted to connect with me.

Seeing none, I start my long drive home to the new gray house with gray walls and wall to wall gray carpet. Gray. Yes, I moved from the nearly torched home that I loved, which by the way was painted a soft rosily pink throughout. Thanks LC for setting my house on fire to punish me for taking great care of your kids. (Some things in life are totally unexplainable.)

Pepper repeat after me: you have the ability to change what you want to change. If the operative word is gray, you have options. Sell the gray car and get a red mom mobile. Paint the coffin gray colored walls something bright – Day Lily yellow and sunrise orange. If you are lonely...well maybe Berry will be in contact. If not, make a list of chores that must get done. Do each one and check it off the list. That always cheers you up. Make things happen for you. If you are feeling like a Zombie, wait until the little kids are asleep and sneak out for a 9:45 movie. Eat popcorn, cry into the rough theatre napkins, and go to bed. Tomorrow is another day of high potential. Picture it, be it. Say trite things, be a trite person. Got it.

And then my purse shivers. My cell phone! Is it Berry? I had been hoping so all day. I had sent Berry an example of my prose and it was at great risk to my fragile ego. Would he recognize himself in the prose or just assume it was part of a story I was writing?

Please read it. What do you think? Was it like super obvious and I'm like a 12-year-old passing notes about some pimply boy who won't have male hormones pulsating in his body for another 3 years?

"Whiskey met rum as they slowly touched lips. They both paused to search each other's eyes for consent, for acknowledgement of matched pleasure. Their sweet innocent press had welcomed the flirtatious to passion. He lowered his eyes to her flushed, full lips and pressed towards her. A whimper escaped her as she fought her instincts to release 15 years of celibacy across a bar table. Timing was essential. She could be rutted tonight – he was eager, gaining strength and insistence. Or she could tame and train him for a night of orgasmic bliss."

I wish I could read your face as you read this. Thoughts? Comments? Suggestions? I wish I could read Berry's face as he read it. Not hearing from him has me in stages of anxiety, dread, mortification.

The evening went without a peep from Georgia. Bile formed. Not in my mouth but like a dervish swill in my mind. Anger was picking up speed like a tornado whisks up houses. I added the following to my paragraph. Take that you breadcrumbing creep.

"Time to choose was quickly fleeing as she was being engulfed in a stronghold of toned arms, chest fur, and baritone murmurs of need. Her castle was to be stormed, his long, steel hard weapon was about to be unsheathed. What could slow his hormonal army?

She heard "rut, rut, rut" in her mind. No longer desirous, just panicky she wanted to stop. This wasn't love. This was an arrogant 64- year-old man who needed speed to ensure his erectile dysfunction wouldn't ruin the party.

Feeling extreme disappointment, her ardor had chilled to ice. Having hoped for love, she found he was just a bastard on a mission to emit his last blast. The months spent cultivating a romance were for naught. There would be no rutting, no lovemaking. In the view of the lonely business travelers drinking at the bar, she felt safe resisting and stopping his advancements."

Yeah Berry. That's what you get for ignoring me all day. Erectile Dysfunction. Go on with your busy self. Party hardy with your right hand. Or are you left-handed?

Therapy Session: Ben & Barbie

Quick Recap:
Ben aged 38, Barbie turning 38 this week. Average, modest dress. Slim builds. Very understated, humble mannered. Ben was a mortgage broker for a medium sized bank and Barbie was a purchasing agent for an international corporation.

Session:
This couple struggles with a delicate issue and I have great respect for their honesty with a stranger (me) and how they are gently finding their way either through or out of the conflict. This is only our second visit, and it was a surprise to see they made the appointment through the online service. (I don't trust the online scheduling app – and long for days with receptionists!) I am hoping I can be of service. They are both educated, philosophical, congenial as a couple. They are parents of a 12-year-old son, whom it appears they both nurture and enjoy.

Married for 13 years, the wife had a dalliance about six months ago. She works with this man in person twice a year and by phone and online daily. At a winter holiday party (company can't call it a Christmas party), she was into the Peppermint White Russians like a pelican dive bombing for fish. Barbie believes she only behaved badly because of the alcohol. Otherwise, she had a perfectly fine marriage.

Ben agrees they have a very satisfying, middle-class lifestyle. Ben accepts that this incident happened and believes Barbie will never break their marriage vows again. Barbie appreciates Ben for his trust in her. Barbie is using the past tense when talking about how well they are coping with this breach in their seemingly stable married life.

It is the "elephant in the room" time. We are now on our second session of pleasantries. What is not being said? What is bringing them to therapy? Before I ask, I always feel whatever the last thing I ate start to rise and enter my mouth at this stage. But I must ask. Why are you here? What is the issue or issues?

Ben inspects my carpet for crumbs, ants, microscopic bugs. Barbie has her eyes raised, begging the ceiling to fall on her. I wait. I can wait all the way to session three. I get paid whether the couple wants to talk, wants to improve something, or not. I have found a place to affix my gaze between them. I mold my face into a kind, confessional priest look. Bit tough to pull off with a short skirt, fake eyelashes, and swinging straight black hair. Wish I had a mirror to see if my contortions are effective. Wish I could sneak a peek to see if Berry has played a new word. Wish I had a Dairy Queen – medium hot fudge sundae.

Possibly I have mentioned that I am incontinent. Years of sitting, waiting, listening and not being able to bolt to the bathroom broke my muscles in ladyland or something medical is malfunctioning. Anyway, I cannot hold it and the signal system we all learned as children, to count on, wore out. So, it is what it is. No one is talking so my body involuntarily uses the silence to fill my diaper. Yep. With luck only the splash kind is eliminated. I hate when a pungent smell explodes on the scene, and we all try to pretend I didn't crap on myself. When this happens, only about once a week, clients tend to solve their issues quickly, stand to leave and promise to schedule online for another session.

Yep. Pretty much the most unappealing 62-year-old woman on the planet. But stellar as a therapist because the clients who witness this seem to be cured as I normally don't see them again.

Ok, Barbie, give it up. The one who looks at the ceiling is the one with the problem. I just know from years of the quiet game. Barbie, I softly speak her name. She responds after inhaling half the oxygen from the room. "I didn't know. I am Catholic. We were virgins when we got married. I didn't have a clue on our wedding night. I had been worried sex would hurt. My mom said I would bleed a little and then it would stop. Ben was great though. He didn't hurt me at all. I never bled. I liked sex with Ben."

Ben has now discovered some algorithm to my carpet fibers. His head is nearly between his legs. Barbie hesitantly continued. "When I got drunk and had relations with my coworker, I was really surprised. He entered me like Ben never did and it was a whole new experience. I really liked it. He was huge and I told him that. But he said he was average size. So, the next day I actually asked a girlfriend and she agreed that 5-6 inches is average."

Silence. Regret hung like tapestries in Gone with the Wind, heavy, clunky, awkward.

Barbie added, "I'm almost 38 years old and I want average. I'm sorry Ben."

Ben took Barbie's hand and looked into her eyes. "I'm so sorry Barbie. I want to be bigger but there is nothing I can do. Can we please work something else out?"

Barbie swung her head back and forth emphasizing no. Ben rose without comment and left my room.

Barbie turned to me. Thank you, Dr. James. I guess we are done here. I stood and felt the soggy diaper drop dangerously close to my hem line. I assured Barbie she was welcome any time, with or without Ben.

I waited about 3 minutes for Barbie to clear my waiting room and then race-waddled to the bathroom. I keep a stash of women's XL disposable underwear duck taped under the sink and was freshened up in no time, just in case you were curious.

Are you interested in more information?

1. Micropenis – an unusually small penis. Micropenis occurs in about 0.6% of males. It is usually less than 3.67 inches when stretched. The condition is caused by hormonal or genetic abnormalities or have no known cause. The Micropenis can still perform and have sexual pleasure. Surgical reconstruction (phalloplasty) in younger children is an option. An adult male can seek medical advice to weigh the risks and benefits for their situation.

2. The internet has information which should be carefully read for fact versus fiction.

3. Couples can have happy marriages and an emphasis on penal size diminishes other strengths and abilities. The bedroom can be a very private, creative space to enjoy the myriad of ways to pleasure each other. Consider seeing a Sex Therapist. They are specially trained in sex therapy methods.

Conversation Starters

Day trip to buy half an alligator, cow, or pig (For Minnesotans – people down south do eat alligator!)

1. Do you think you have perfect imperfections?
   What are some of them?

2. If you could have just one talent and the rest of what you did was super lousy, what would you like your talent to be? Why?

3. What age that ends in a zero, has you most excited
   (for good or bad) and why?

4. How would you like for me to romance you? What could I do?

5. Is there a hobby or interest of yours, you wish I cared about more or wished I worked with you on?

Chapter Eight

I am leaving Minnesota soon. My little grandchildren have left my home for their father's. I have cleaned the house top to bottom. The laundry basket is empty (for at least 10 seconds). My sweet St. Bernard has plenty of food and treats. Dishwasher running, sink clean. My luggage is in the car. I am leaving on a writer's retreat for 11 days.

Or am I? I declined to tell anyone where I was flying to. I referred to Star Hollow, the magical little town the show Gilmore Girls was set in. But the magic I want is in Dublin, Georgia. I am crossing the country to catch glimpses of Berry running, entering his workplace, mowing his lawn. I promise I will not try to contact him. I just have this urgent need to be closer to him.

Is this stalking behavior? Am I an unwelcome visitor? Please read the following Messenger exchange and judge me gently.

To set the scene, Berry had just asked for a video chat. I drove to a school parking lot in the mother van, parked. I was safe, it was 4:30 and very few cars were left. No family to run out and ruin the call. No one around. The camera went on and there he was. The sexy smile, kind eyes, masculinity zooming. He was at his office desk, sitting back, legs apart. Oh, yum-yum.

My heart has a rhythm that beats to "Hallelujah" – Susan Boyle's beautiful version. My hands shake. I must keep the cell phone camera up to minimize my face and hide the jowls. I also must work the angles to try to hide my fat arms, so Berry doesn't see the rolls of blubber from my shoulders.

We talked about a fantasy I had. I described being in Dublin as a surprise. Being the sexy, but sensitive woman I am, I had made a little white gift bag up. In it was a mini Glenlivet whiskey and a Captain Morgan rum. Note the reference to the romantic paragraph I had sent him. Berry was a whiskey drinker and I, a rum drinker. I had enclosed a note: Interested in a Happy Hour?

The note was unsigned. I was going to leave the present by his office door one morning before he got to work. And then just drive back to the hotel and do my writing gig and wait.

If Berry wanted to meet, great. If he did not respond or responded that he could not, I would have my answer. Answer to what, you ask. Answer to the "elephant in the room" question: do you want to meet and move the relationship forward?

After I finished describing my little scenario, I looked at Berry. Oh dear.

I could tell Berry was quite uncomfortable. The first thing he said he thought of when he saw the bag was to call the police. Yikes. Why would a gigantic man get that spooked by a gift bag?

Berry recovered his composure and began to play out what he would do, getting into his role as a sex machine dying for a tryst on his office desk. It was great fun and he had oodles of ideas of how to pleasure me. The first picture to arrive was his manly desk, computer monitor, papers, all cleared off. He sent me a picture of his joystick in its most joyful form.

Such fun – until the school principal pulled up next to my car and asked if I was okay.

What? How can this keep happening to our Facetime calls? I can't Facetime in the house because there is no privacy. I tried to Facetime in the van parked in my driveway and the kids found me and pounded on my locked van door. I tried to park a couple blocks down the street and one of my daughters walked the dog past me and gave me a stink eye. Now, I drive over 3 miles away, park away from the building, mind my own business and the freaking principal personally has to stop and question me. Incredible.

Dang it. We ended the call. Berry was quite deflated, or in the process of deflating. He texted me: Your smile is a delight, your eyes incredible. How great to see you! About 20 minutes later he sent me a picture of himself shirtless, just his work pants on. I was in heaven.

But the fantasy had been a test to see if Berry was interested in meeting me. He had played the game, grown extremely amorous, but was he wanting more? So, I texted him.

Me: *So...elephant in the room question...may I ask you something?*

Berry: *Sure*

Me: *On a scale of 0 to 10 with 0 meaning never and 10 meaning extremely interested, how do you feel about an in-person meeting?*

Berry: *It pains you say, but I owe you honesty. I fantasize about it, but morally, I can't think about it seriously.*

Me: *Honesty is welcome. Thank you.*

Berry: *You're welcome.*

There was no air in the room after I read this. My eyes brimmed with tears. Because of the typo or sentence structure I was not sure what he had written. I wrote down some questions. Do you understand what he wrote or is it a bit confusing to you as well?

1. It pains me you say – does Berry mean, he is pained that I asked the question?
2. It pains me you say – does Berry mean, he is pained to have to say...
3. But morally – what? Dick pictures, cybersex that burns up our cell phones it is so hot is morally okay. Meeting is not "morally" okay?

4. Am I just free-porn for Berry? All he wants is an occasional online sex affair. He really doesn't care about my life. I am not an actual person with feelings?

5. What?

I robotically service my family. The sun has dropped from the sky. I will put one foot in front of the other like the soldier of solitude I am. No one will know that my heart stopped beating.

Please note the professional and courteous response I gave when I received Berry's answer. There was no begging, meltdown, rage, protests, arguments. I am a gentlewoman and discretion is essential in my career. Berry had once said his motto was "never let them see you sweat". Ditto baby. I am a professional.

And with the exterior appearance of robot, mechanical mom, and mantra of I am a professional, I am a professional, repeat after me, I am a professional, I took several days off from WWF. I had purchased my flight tickets, booked a hotel 5.6 miles from his home. I had this unique opportunity to write a full book. Not in the five years of becoming a custodial grandparent to my two littles had I had a respite of more than 2 days. This was an extraordinary opportunity to write. And now I could not meet the beacon of my lighthouse. Now that was all shades of wrong.

I had so many thoughts and feelings jumbled. I did what I tell clients to do – I wrote them down. No editing. Just quick writing without regard to sentence structure or making sense. I had 48 entries within about 30 minutes. I broke the tips off two pens I pressed so hard as I wrote. I felt better. And the best part was it was private. I did not need to rant to a girlfriend or sister. I could be myself and let it all leak out without censorship.

As you can imagine, many of the entries surrounded themes such as anger at being used, despair, tsunami waves of depression and hopelessness, self-reproach. And the concept of morality.

Want to read some of the actual entries? The first cluster – the first that came to mind were about relief. Did you expect that? Me neither!

1. Relief. I am incontinent and am not sure
   how I was going to hide this.

2. Relief. I am 5 feet tall and fat. He is 6'4 and
   runs 10 miles several times a week.

3. In contrast, my exercise routine is to apply mashed potatoes to
   my butt, pecan pie to my thighs, generously rub chocolate cake
   to my belly, snort butter and swim in gravy several times a week.

4. Relief. I live a complicated enough life.

5. Morally best.

Watch the progression of venting – almost like the Kubler Ross Stages of Grief.

The above talked about denial – it was never going to work out anyway because I am so defective.

Anger, stage two, rears its ugly head:

1. Ruined writing vacation

2. Berry cut my lifeline – now what?

3. Berry led me on with compliments and pictures

4. He is an asshole pervert who likes to show his dick.

5. I must block him on WWF and Facebook and Messenger.

6. He must have erectile dysfunction and can only masturbate.
   He doesn't want a real woman.

Bargaining:

1. Please let me make it to tomorrow. Thank you, God.
   Keep me moving, keep me alive.

2. If I sit through my sad feelings, I will get through this.

3. If I lost some weight, he would want me.

4. I think I am okay with being a cybersex girlfriend
   because life is better with him in it.

5. Maybe I should send him Esther Perel's book, "The State of Affairs".
   It might help him see the benefits of an affair.

Depression:

1. Life is so dismal. What is there to save me?

2. I have been turned to stone.

3. Sad

4. Betrayed

5. Tired

6. Spiritless

7. Fucked. My heart is fucked.

8. Hate myself for believing someone like Berry
   would be interested in me.

9. Tearless crying.

Acceptance:

1. I was just someone for when he was bored or lonely.
2. He is just not into me. Thank you, God for this book.
3. Why would I accept less than full love? What is behind my history of resigning to less and giving more?
4. Berry's marriage has a huge hole. It is his problem to resolve.
5. God has a plan for me. "Jeremiah 29:11 "For I know the plans I have for you," declares the Lord, "plans to prosper you and not to harm you, plans to give you hope and a future."

Pretty effective technique- heh? At any rate after a few days, I was calm, more logical and started to play WWF against Berry. Nothing more was said about the situation. I resolved to accept the breadcrumbs. I chose to keep his lifeline. I vowed to keep trying to nurture myself and make sure I was not entirely depleted by my familial and professional responsibilities.

Something was better than nothing. Taking a view from 30,000 feet above the earth, I could see we were mutually using each other. He wanted scintillating episodes and to demonstrate his protruding third leg. I needed a text from an uber handsome man who didn't know I was an aging, vain, simpleton with a degenerative spine and cumbersome bowel issues. Deal? Deal.

Therapy Session: Gladys

Quick Recap:

A pleasant daughter gingerly holds arm of her mother, Gladys, and glides her to a chair. Very modest, quiet pair. This is my first session with them.

Session:

My morning client, Gladys, is a remarkable 88-year-old woman. She lives with her 42-year-old daughter who brought her to therapy, dropped her off and raced for a coffee, scone, and peace.

Gladys was started on an antidepressant by her psychiatrist, and I am providing medication monitoring over the next 90 days to make sure she is improving. I have many clients that I collaborate with their psychiatrist. It is an effective partnership. I have the time to monitor the clients and report faithfully to the psychiatrist their status. The psychiatrist can see more clients if I do the follow-up.

Gladys' history described her as a lively extrovert who enjoyed going to her community center's senior activities. The winter in Minnesota had been especially brittle cold and she had not gotten out as much. Her skin was mottled grey. She was slouched on my stuffed chair. Her voice was nearly inaudible. She was on day 5 of her medication. Incredibly sad countenance.

My voice lowered to match hers. I couldn't quite discern what she was saying. I asked if I could hold her hand and she offered hers, translucent, bony, and long fingered. I asked if she would like some lavender lotion and she nodded. I massaged some lotion on her hand with whispery strokes – as though I was petting a butterfly. I asked if she could smell the lavender. She could not.

I was evaluating Gladys while offering her human touch. I was concerned with anosmia, a loss of smell in the elderly. Seniors over 80 years old can experience a significant reduction in the sense of smell. This can impact their safety and nutritional status. It also may indicate nasal or sinus problems and even nasal polyps. Or, Alzheimer's and Parkinson's disease might be causing the loss of smell.

I started to mentally enumerate a list of questions for Gladys' daughter. The chief concern was Gladys' safety as she would not necessarily smell a fire. How many hours a day is Gladys alone in the house as the daughter works? Is there an adult day program that Gladys could attend so that she is creatively engaged and has social interactions?

Gladys offered me her other hand. I happily gooped it up. Gladys was looking at me through her white pupiled eyes. She had well developed cataracts. I wondered if her daughter realized the cataracts might be contributing to Gladys depression as she might not be seeing well at all. Cataract surgery is a quick miracle and might give Gladys better vision and increase her safety walking around, seeing her craft projects, cooking, etc.

Not much was said between Gladys and me. Yet I was thrilled to have a flood of ideas to offer Gladys and her daughter. Life simply did not have to be this difficult. I am not a social worker, which I believe Gladys could use. However, resource development is a vital service I offer. Gladys left with recommendations for a gerontologist, an ophthalmologist for her cataract evaluation, adult day centers in their community, transportation services for the elderly and some home volunteer projects to bring Gladys back to feeling vital and needed.

Are you interested in more information?

1. Anosmia: Bring your loved one to a doctor if you suspect they are losing their sense of smell. Whatever may be causing this can possibly be corrected. Long term anosmia may cause nutrition issues ranging from adding salt or sugar to amplify taste, to a disinterest in eating. It may lead to lack of hygiene and related changes in self-care.
2. Cataracts: Cause clouded or blurred vision, double vision, difficulty seeing during the night, difficulty driving at night, sensitivity to light and glare, need for brighter than normal lights to read or see objects, seeing halo around lights, seeing life as faded or washed in a yellow color, eye pain, headaches due to changes in vision.
3. Have your loved one see an ophthalmologist who specializes in cataracts. Do not accept this condition as normal. There are ways to restore vision.

Conversation Starters

Grocery and TP Run
(eating the first will cause the need for the second)

1. Pickles, tuna fish, or jalapenos – which one would you choose if you had to eat one of the with every meal the rest of your life? Why?
2. What are 5 qualities you cannot stand in a person?
3. What are 5 qualities every person should have to make the world a better place?
4. If heaven could send back one person to live a few more years, who would you choose? Why?
5. Do you think you could achieve your life goals if given one last year to make it happen? Why? What would need to happen to achieve them?

Chapter Nine

I am still flying to Atlanta and driving south to Dublin. I do not plan to drop off any white bags or contact him in any manner. I do plan to write and pray and sort out what kinda nutso I am. Meanwhile, Berry has resumed texting. Today's is another riotous sexy escapade. Berry loves to write bodice-ripping scenarios! As do I!

Berry: *A smile rises to his lips as he savors the feel of her hand on his package.*

Leaning on his desk. (Berry sends an updated picture of his desk).

Me: *That's a fine desk for a rut fest!!!*

Berry: *Right?*

His fingers now reach to explore her

Me: *Desk of my dreams. May she slide his pants down?*

Berry: (Sends a picture of his happy lower limb.)

His member dangling, she drops his drawers.

And his smile grows.

Me: *She smiles and wants to lick and eat. She calls herself an Oral Explorer.*

Berry: *Let's reverse positions*

He pulls a pillow from his chair and places it behind her ass.

Pulls off the black sundress and forces her back into the pillow, papers on the desk go flying.

He's on his knees now, her smooth legs parted wide

His middle finger and tongue converge at her slit

As she moaned softly

Me: *Her urgency to lavish his staff with warm, firm pressure is overcoming her...*

Berry: *He puts his plans on hold, as her hand grabs his organ, it's clear he must go wherever she wants to steer him*

Around the desk she guides him

Her mouth takes him inside its warmth and now he's moaning.

Me: *Such a beautiful cock. Absolutely delicious. She is beyond joy... the sight of him extended and engorged is her favorite.*

Berry: *She takes in his length, and he can think of nothing better than being deep inside her warmth*

He has an idea, not sure if it will work

He wants to taste her while she continues to suck.

Me: *She lifts her green eyes in surprise as he guides her to 69 on the floor.*

Berry: *His lips and finger meet at her crease once again. His tongue lightly laps at her bud from below as his finger finds it from above.*

Me: *Breathing heavily, she rocks back from her oral adorations to enjoy a heat rising from her ladyland.*

Berry: *His tongue now drawn to her lips, he continues pressure on her nub, while his other hand now explores her fine behind. The three sources of pleasure now work together, and his senses are on fire. He's rock hard now and can think of nothing but burying himself deep and deeper. The image of her on his desk, dark tanned skin, legs open and parted wide is all he can see.*

Me: *Her need has her slippery wet, hot, verging on exploding. Saying his name in a low, raspy, needful moan…he has been welcomed to heaven's gate. Enter.*

Berry: *He imagines a searing sound as his hardness approaches her tenderness.*

Me: *She bites her lip as she feels her tight muscles stretch to accommodate his magnificent manhood. Exhaling wondrous passion, wordless happiness*

Berry: *His Corona parts her lips and he feels a moist, wet, warm pleasure meeting his approach. In a split second it's at the bottom of her channel. Urgently seeking a deeper bottom. He moves close to the desk and his hands grab her luscious cheeks pulling them deeper onto his cock in one motion. As he raises himself up to rub against her nub, he glides in and out. The sound of twin moaning dissipates into the empty office.*

Me: *Quieting her need to call out her pleasure, she burrows into his chest, taking nibbles of his nipples. Waves of tightening tremble thru her core. He knows how to please a woman and her responses reward his efforts.*

Berry: *And he feels the tightening, which excites him even more. He's a driven man now, plunging, squeezing, kissing, licking, fingers exploring and cock rising and falling. She has him frenzied and he knows he can't last long at this pace.*

Me: *Her desire is to please him. When he is ready, she will hold on for his explosion and not release until every drop has been shot into her cavern.*

Berry: *The explosion mounts. The tightening of her muscles around his shaft add to the pressure and pleasure. Pace of plunging quicken. Seems to be deeper with every second. I can't hold any longer. Letting go. Deeply inserted in the hole.*

Me: *Deeper, she pants…I want everything…yes. Yes. Yes.*

Berry: (sends an audio clip of him moaning)

Me: *Omg you sound awesome*

Berry: *Imagining your ladyland makes me feel awesome.*

(Berry sends a dick pic of a most incredible 6+ inches and wide girth.)

Me: *You literally make me want to lick my phone…good god Berry. It is so good.*

Berry: *Your wonderful sense of expression has made a real mess of things here. Hope you're proud of yourself.*

Me: *It was so good for me…and the visual was beyond a dream… so I am more satiated than proud. You give good sex.*

Berry: *And so, do you*

Berry: *Gotta get back to work. Later Mon Ami.*

Me: *Adios*

Well. I hope you enjoyed reading this. Would you like to discuss how moral this cybersex is? I was raised Catholic. Doing something wrong is a sin. But if you even think it, it is a sin. If you text it with pictures, I am certain that is a sin too. So, if you were me, how would you regard Berry's "but morally, I can't think about it seriously" statement? I think there is a lot of concern, a lot of issues he must be struggling with. I will extend grace to him.

These are very confusing times. We all need to extend more grace, understanding and kindness. Especially when it comes to a man who loves to write out his fantasies! By the way, did you notice Berry slipped from 3rd person to speaking of himself when he wrote, "I can't hold it any longer".

What a guy!

Therapy Session: Leslie

Quick Recap:

Soft, messy curls in her short hair, thick glasses with a frame that was needing replacement soon. Sweatshirt and sweatpants, tennis shoes. Large purse pulling her right shoulder down. If you want to see the face of an overworked angel, it is Leslie's.

Session:

Leslie is a custodial grandparent of a 15-year-old, twin 7-year-old boys, and a newborn addicted to cocaine. She is 71 years old and her spouse, the step-grandparent is 76. The biological parents of the children are her daughter and son and whoever they slept with. I rarely see Leslie as she is so occupied with caring for her grandchildren. Leslie is welcome with little notice needed. I do not charge Leslie. Her well-being is more important than money. And she is critically short of both.

The courts transferred parental rights to Leslie for each child after the parents continued their drug use and neglect. The newborn was born and suffers cocaine addiction because Leslie's daughter used regularly during her pregnancy. The older kids are medically and academically challenged.

Leslie and her spouse are struggling with their health. Leslie has had a lifetime with Rheumatoid Arthritis and her spouse has prostrate, skin and colon cancer. No matter, their home was deemed the safest for the children.

Leslie comes mostly to release her heartache and frustration in long diatribes. I let her vent. I do not problem solve with her. I have learned not to research resources. She is alone doing heroic work that people half her age could not do. I provide Diet Coke by the liter, a comfy chair, a thick, plush blanket, a towel warmed in my microwave for her cold hands, soft lighting, and my admiration.

It helps Leslie to walk through her extraordinary but typical day and hear me express incredulousness, praise, prayers, and disbelief as appropriate. Once we tried to create a circle of support to identify respite possibilities. Leslie seemed to have no one. No neighbor, no church affiliation, no social worker, no healthy children sans alcohol, drugs, and criminal behavior. Leslie became sadder and the exercise was clearly wrong for her. My bad. I have learned that some people don't want help, they just want to talk and find their own way. I can do this.

Leslie joined Grandparents as Parents (G.A.P.S) which is an online support group. She writes late at night of the day's struggles and other grandparents make comments. This has been a powerful outreach tool for her. As a custodial grandparent of two myself, I can deeply acknowledge her fatigue, worry and frustrations. But I keep my mouth shut. Leslie needs to hear herself think out loud.

Leslie sighs deeply, "Just worn out. More than tired. Having such a hard time thinking about the future. My adopted granddaughter is 15 tomorrow. I'm not having a party. I don't have the energy to even make her a cake...when my own daughter was growing up, I made a big deal of birthdays -invited her class over, made treat bags. Now, I don't even have a gift ready. Got no money for a gift...suppose I should go to Goodwill and see if anything looks new enough for a gift. Her dad, my son, is going to be 36 and if he has any money, he'll be buying an 8 ball of shit. He don't care if he breaks probation. She cares. When he stays overnight, she thinks it's a party. I won't let him sleep at my house if he's high. She don't need to see her daddy all stupid. He gets mean too. I gotta protect her..."

Leslie leaves after almost downing the full liter of Diet Coke. She was heard, acknowledged, praised, reinforced, and warmed. She will come again – sooner is better. But Leslie knows what she needs and when she wants to meet her own needs. I give Leslie a bottle of Diet Coke for the road and a poetic letter I found that touched my heart and I hoped it would hers.

Dear Grandparent.

I want you to know that I see you.

I see you running your grandchild to therapy when your friends are running to their nail salon appointment.

I see you dropping off your grandchild at school and attending yet another IEP meeting, while your friends are having coffee.

I see you slipping out the of conversation when your friends are all chiming in about golfing, traveling, and visiting grandchildren.

I see you juggling appointments and meetings, always making sure you do the best for your grandchild.

I see you sitting at your computer for hours researching what your grandchild needs.

I see you at the end of the day, thoroughly spent and exhausted.

I see you rocking a baby, chasing a toddler, reading to a first grader, learning the new math with a 10-year-old, trying to understand the new lingo with your 8th grade, fearfully teaching a 16-year-old how to drive, and preparing college forms with your senior. I see you.

I see you cringe when people whine about the petty things that pale in comparison to your day.

I see you spread thin, but still going the extra mile for your grandchild, and managing to do it with a smile.

I see you digging for depths of strength you never dreamed you had.

I see you rubbing out the arthritis pain and trying to keep up with a slight limp in your gait.

I see the pain in your eyes when all you do is taken for granted and you are the only one, they can lash out on. You stay stoic, unwavering, and strong for them.

I see the comfort in your arms as you comfort their pain, but there are no arms to comfort you.

I see you showing appreciation to the teachers, therapists and medical professionals and all who reach out to help your grandchild.

I see you reluctantly rising early in the morning to do all over again after another chaotic night.

I see you when you are hanging on to dear life at the end of your rope.

I know you feel invisible, like nobody notices any of it. But I want you to know I notice you. I see you in the trenches, relentlessly pushing forward. I see you worrying about failing this child. I see you grieving your own child. I see you quietly blaming yourself for their failures and choices.

What I want you to know is – it's worth it. On days when you wonder if you can do it another minute, I want you to know that I see you. I want you to know you are beautiful. I want you to know you are not alone. There are thousands of us, silently doing what we know is best. I want you to know that love is what matters the most. Your love.

And on those days when you see your grandchild smile, when you hear their laughter, watch them succeed in life – know it was all worth it. I will see you then too and I want you to know I am proud of you.

Anonymous

Do you want more information?

1. Grandparents as Parents (G.A.P.S) can be found on Facebook under groups.
2. www.nacac.org is the website for The North American Council on Adoptable Children. Their website lists support groups for grandparents as well as other resources for strengthening families.
3. www.aarp.org/online-community offers information for raising grandchildren
4. Each state has a GrandFacts facts sheet to find out what resources are available. www.grandfactsheets.org
5. Grandparents Raising Children Support Group is at www.dailystrength.org

Conversation Starters

Folding and Sorting Laundry Mountain

1. What 5 rules for life would you give a young person?
2. Have you experienced a small thing that made a great impact?
3. If you could star in a movie, what movie, and what role?
4. Name 3 pet peeves.
5. How well do you think you can fake being nice? How well would you friends say do at faking?

Chapter Ten

I am in Dublin, Georgia. What a cute town. Better than Star Hollow of Gilmore fame. And the charming Dublin is not a crime hamlet from appearances. Just a town of 16,000 hard-working people. I have found my hotel which is one of a newish chain. The reason I chose to stay at this hotel is the manmade lake on the backside. My room faces the lake, and I moved my writing desk to oversee the swans and watch the ripples of water. It is perfect for contemplation.

I spent my first evening finding Berry's house. His plantation is way off the road. I cannot see it from the street and Google Earth just finds dense trees and marks it as his address. I have not found the Caribbean restaurant he mentioned eating lunch at. If I can find it, I know he works nearby because in one of his texts he mentioned slipping next door for Caribbean BBQ. I am aware this reads as if I were a true stalker. I am not ashamed. Yet.

Less you do think I am stalking, well define stalking. I do not want to meet him because of his response. I have spent most of my time in the hotel room writing. It is when I go for food, I take a couple of drives around. I do not want to interrupt his life, I just would love to see him run on the railroad tracks...you know, innocent things like that. Is that crazy on the rise?

Word of advice to you all. Do not try to be a successful marriage and family therapist and juggle an online affair with a married man. The two activities are working at opposite goals. One helps couples stay together and the other dangerously lures a deeply committed married man into a tempting, lurid adventure. Just because I thought I could does not mean I should.

Am I a psycho stalker or simply an enamored online lover that hates being spurned and then re-ignited? Like a game of Torrid Breadcrumbing. Pepper James, welcome to having an affair where the intelligent but morally wayward have to accept these lapses in contact without complaint. After all, the person who accepts their role in an affair, automatically accepts being number 2 in the other person's life. Or number 5 in lines of affection or further down the love chain depending on how many women are in queue.

I have been breadcrumbed to starvation. Just as Hansel and Gretel thought they would find their way home if they left breadcrumbs, the breadcrumb-ee follows breadcrumbs with heightened hope that they will find their way to the center of the breadcrumber's heart. Think of not having enough connection, enough love, enough commitment to really be in a relationship. But you, the breadcrumb-ee, have accepted crumbs of compliments, occasional attention, maybe a late-night booty call. All in the extreme delusion that all the breadcrumbs will constitute a whole loaf. Nope. Will not. You may have the ingredients to make a complete loaf, but the oven doesn't work. Or the ingredients are stale. Or the baker really wants a donut, not bread but is just hungry and eats anything. Or the breadcrumber leaves breadcrumbs for several online women and just likes to see which starving recipient finds him first.

Now, I am educated. I am licensed as a marriage and family therapist. I am not as young as I think I am. I should know the classic signs of non-interest. It is just that I cannot believe I am being strung along. After all, I am wonderful and have tons to offer him. Sadly, I also am aware that should Berry meet me and I am not the French Maid outfit wearing, long-legged, tanned and toned, big bosomed, red high heel wearing babe, and if he rejects me…well, I will be rejected. Without him getting to know me.

I want to be known and found loveable just as I am. Do you think I should wait until near the end of my trip and text him that I am passing through town, and can he meet for just a whiskey and rum? Am I pathetic? I believe so too.

Therapy Session: Olive

Quick Recap:
Probable diagnosis of Adjustment Disorder – coping with new motherhood, relationship problems. Chief coping strategy: overeating.

Session:
Olive sits down precisely in the center of my comfy chair. She has an earnest face – kind of like a puppy hoping to figure out what its owner wants. She tells me she likes my earrings, necklace, shoes, scarf, something...she always has a pleasantry to share. The circles under her eyes are dark and I assume she had tried makeup to cover them up, but the product failed. I wonder about the darkness – is this a sleep problem or dehydration symptom? Olive removes from her purse her friend and mine, a Diet Coke.

Cheers, I say to her as we tap bottles. Chin-chin I hear Berry saying in my head. Time for Berry to leave my head. I must work.

How is life, I ask Olive. I do not have an agenda for Olive. One analogy is that she has many irons in the fire, but hers are made of tissue paper and many catch on fire at the same time. Olive says brightly in this voice that I recognize to be as fake as my hair color, "fine". I laugh and smile. We both know that FINE can stand for Freaked out, Insecure, Neurotic and Emotional.

Another acronym for FINE is Frantic, Insane, Nuts and Egotistical. Or Faithful, Involved, Knowledgeable and Experienced. My personal favorite is Feeling I'm Nothing to Everyone.

Olive is 32 years old, married and a mother through adoption from Haiti. She is the household breadwinner, the household maid, the household laundress, cook, lawn mower, tree trimmer and less than proud spouse of a minimally employed "mama's boy". Her descriptions, not mine. I would sum up Olive's FINE as Feelings Inside Not Expressed.

Olive is over 100 pounds beyond her high school weight, and she is miserable. FLEAS – Feelings Largely Eaten And Swallowed. Olive hopes counseling will help her get her weight under control. Good job connecting food with counseling. Food can be such a crutch. Dairy Queens are more dangerous than taverns to some of us.

The acronyms of AA appeal to Olive. They are a safe way to describe succinctly what she is experiencing, as well as provide her a short mantra to use for coping. For example, Olive will talk in guarded terms about her husband and conclude with CRAP. Carry Resentments Against People. She says to herself, let go of the CRAP. She has learned to follow this with DETACH – Don't Even Think About Changing Him.

Olive likes to talk about her 3-year-old from Haiti. He is making great progress. She loves this little dude, and accepts the stress of teaching toileting, hygiene, table etiquette, English, manners and so much more. Little dude was a street toddler who was placed in an orphanage. Scrappy, distrustful, overwhelmed…lots going on for him being in America.

Olive is worried about her newest 11-pound weight gain. It had a super-fast onset.

I am worried about it too. Everything appears so out of control for Olive – her work is demanding, motherhood is demanding, marriage is demanding. Even the best acronyms can't wrestle all this, all the time. GIFT – God Is There Forever. Olive is a Christian which gives her some hope of better times.

As I listen, I start jotting down thoughts: Cortisol, the stress hormone; daycare or respite care possible? Establish a date night and weekday night to herself? Can we develop routine selfcare, and a nutritionist? Is there a Vitamin D deficiency or a need for a referral for an anti-depressant? Would a Myers Briggs Inventory show her unique strengths? Perhaps encourage a girlfriend night, church involvement, or marriage counseling?

Olive likes to image- manage most of her worries. This is something that she might say, "Little dude tried to stab me with a fork this morning. Poor dude, so much to learn and the proper way to use silverware is just one more thing." Or "My mom is working on adjusting to being a grandmother. She is telling her neighbors all about my infertility and how there were no white babies in Haiti."

To address specifically where to start when every sentence Olive speaks opens another can of whoop-ass problems, I try to see if there is a desire to prioritize them for change, or if just talking helps. Olive is wary of prioritizing for change. Talking was enough. Ok, starting where Olive wants to start, I just ask the magic wand question. She can answer immediately or take it home as homework and return later to discuss.

Magic Wand Question: Olive, of all that you juggle and balance remarkably well, what is one thing that a magic wand could make better and really help you? Olive's face is dark and gloomy. I can tell she does not trust the question. I sit and wait through her discomfort and processing. She remains silent.

I gesture as though to give her the magic wand. "This is your wand that is preprogrammed to improve whatever you touch with it. Would you like to share what you want to touch first or bring it home for homework?"

She starts to repeatedly touch her upper thighs. "I want to change my weight. I have got to lose 100 pounds." I nod. "The magic wand will respond to your request. How will you start this magic?"

Olive looks mystified. I ask to brainstorm with her. Oh. Light bulb on. Brain registered. Olive starts describing what she has done that has failed. I give her a limited time for this and ask to break into her monologue. FEAR – Failure Expected And Received. Olive brightens. This woman loves her some acronyms! Let's start with the basic magic of weight loss. A full physical with blood tests for Vitamin D and other levels. Testing for Cortisol, a primary stress hormone. A doctor's recommendation for a nutritionist.

Can you accomplish this magic before our next appointment? Olive agrees. Olive has the magic wand. I give Olive one more parting gift: the acronym HALT – Hungry, Angry, Lonely, Tired: Fix these situations before you eat. Olive goes for a hug. I give her my best professional hug, which is basically a thank you for the hug. You will do great. Goodbye-hug.

Are you interested in more information?

1. Acronyms from AA: https://club12.org/reference/aa-acronyms

Conversation Starters

Child-Free Conversation Starts (Don't forget you were a couple before his Highness, or her Highness appeared)

1. What makes you feel super sexy?
2. What are some of the most pleasant sensations for you? (All senses count)
3. If you had married via an arranged marriage, who would your parents have chosen and why?
4. If you could without being caught, where would you like to have a little fun?
5. What are you most sentimental about from our past together? Any memory or a memento?

Chapter Eleven

Today is day 9 in Dublin. I leave Georgia in two days. I never caught sight of Berry jogging-running, never found his office nor the Caribbean Barbeque restaurant. Never caught him leaving his palatial home in the woods. I have driven to every googled restaurant that mentions BBQ. Cannot find any office space he might be renting "next door".

This morning I did come up with one possibility. I have driven up and down the street of his home. There is no shoulder to park on. Nowhere to hide. However, if he heads out to work, turns towards the town area, there is a church yard I could park on, facing the intersection. I would need binoculars to see if he is the driver. The yard has a 20-foot dirt path on it where I could park. If I can get the make of his car, and if I hustle, (trying not to rip up the lawn) I might be able to follow him into town and see where he works.

If I see where he works, I can find somewhere to catch him at noon running on the railroad tracks and then my life would be complete. Right? Absolutely cuckoo? Right? That's the plan. Yep. Gonna get my Berry fix.

Excuse me? I am sensing criticism. Frankly, I have been just the epitome of restraint. In the 9 days of being here I have done what I had to do – write, pray, diet, leave my chin hairs alone. An enormous show of self-control. Surely you agree.

So here is the situation. Here is what I am not able to restrain myself from: I want to text an invitation to meet for a drink. There is a not entirely awful looking bar next to my hotel, The Blue Stag Tavern. It shares the hotel's manmade lake. We could meet. One drink. I go back to Minnesota happy or rejected and mortified. If I am rejected, he can cross me off his list of free cybersex chicks. If rejected, it is over at any rate. I pray I will let it be over. But I will have at least earned points because I showed bravery and faced my fears of rejection.

Let's say he rejects me. He has his wife and family. I go back to indentured servitude and prepare my book for submissions to publishers. We never meet or play Scrabble again with each other. A life of quiet desperation continues for me. Maybe my book gets published and helps a few people. That would be awesome. All will be as it shall be.

Do you agree? Is this the plan? Would you do it if you were me? Oh, and I have another question to ask of you. I wonder, regardless of what happens – rejection or acceptance, if I should tell his wife? Should Berry's wife know her husband is cruising online and populating the planet with pics of his schlong? What are your thoughts on this?

I am very conflicted. I am a woman. I have been cheated on by both husbands (probably while I was washing their damn undies and washing their damn dishes). I suspect Berry is experienced in many forms of cybersex and maybe his dick pics are in a gallery, and he is just sending one of many from his Phallus Folder.

Woman to woman, does she need to know? I would not have appreciated hearing about my ex's exploits, but if it jump-started a divorce and saved me years of being breadcrumbed within my own home, yes tell me. If she already knows and has accepted that her dog leaves the porch, what is another contact from animal control?

Your opinion counts.

Let's vote on each single issue.

Vote One: Should I contact Berry?

Argument for yes:

I feel like cybersex is already adultery. So, what is a chance at being rutted by an enormous stallion after 16 years of celibacy worth, sin wise? Does hell have a step program where a cybersex adulteress is closer to hell's front door where it might be a tad cooler? Does an in-person adulteress spend eternity deeper in the furnace room, amidst excruciating flames?

I am hearing a resounding yes to inviting for a drink. Here is the plan: One little drink. I will check out the bar and find a table with the most flattering lights or the least unflattering shadows. I will practice walking to the table without my walker or cane and see how badly I limp and how desperate I am to hold onto something. Or maybe I will get there early and be seated so Berry does not see the palsy, arthritic show.

I am going to try and go without a diaper. Sorry, Silhouette and all the manufacturers that think pink diapers with black faded inked bows are sexy. Once you put a pad in that pink gauze that can absorb 8 gallons of pee, sexy it is not. Reversely, the "sexier" the diaper, the less product it holds should one become incontinent with more than a tablespoon from zone 1 or zone 2.

Just a personal aside to diaper manufacturers – just because a woman may need an adult diaper does not mean she is a sexless crone that is happy to sit on basically a pillow crammed down her pants. Is there not one thing invented that is ultra-absorbent without being the size of a Volkswagen Bug?

I will groom ladyland and pray that if it gets used, it will not shower the man or worse, leak a stench and brown streak on the sheets. So much to go wrong if I get "lucky".

Oh well. I am just a dreamer and a worrier. What is the worst that can happen? Plenty. But a thought bubble pops up and I console myself with the memory of when my client Amy readily admitted she farted while being licked like a popsicle down there. I almost fell out of my chair trying not to laugh. And although I did not bust into gales of giggling, I did wet myself. Of course.

So yeah. Things happen during sex. And in my case, things that might send Berry galloping back to his wife and living the white gallon hat life for all his living days. Another benefit to having sex with Berry. I will be a huge turnoff and restore his marriage. I am altruistic like that.

Now, for the second question. Should I tell his wife about her naked gardener sending his zucchini pics? I kinda sense a no being whispered through the hotel window from an appalled universe. Ok. Got it.

Wish me luck. I text Berry.

Me: *Hi Berry! How's your day been?*

Berry: *I am blessed with work. Yours?*

Me: *Good. I am almost finished with my book and wondered if you wanted to join me for a celebratory drink?*

Berry: *Facetime Happy Hour?*

Me: *Or I was thinking of meeting at the Blue Stag Tavern.*

Berry: *What?*

Me: *Do you know where it is?*

Berry: *Yes, but why do you know?*

Me: *I am in town today and tomorrow and just wondered.*

Berry: *Pepper?*

Me: *Yes, sir?*

Berry: *Remember what I said about meeting?*

Me: *Yes, I do. And I certainly understand if you do not want to.*
It is just a thought.

Berry: *I am surprised. I don't know how to answer you.*

Me: *No worries. Text me either way please.*

Berry: (sad emoji)

Oh boy. That did not go well. He might be mad. I am a bit shaky. What have I done? Wonder if I screwed things up forever? Tragic Pepper talking. Where is logical Pepper? Come out Logical Pepper. You just caught him way by surprise.

It is okay. It is okay either way. God has the plan. Breathe. Do something constructive. Pack your suitcases. You can leave tonight and drive closer to Atlanta for your flight. You might be done here. One small step at a time. Stay busy, Pepper, pull yourself together.

I methodically put one foot in front of the other. I sit at my desk, googling on the laptop for Atlanta hotels close to the airport. I have my phone on the charger, so I do not miss a text. Ok then. You can do this Pepper. See. Now I have a back-up hotel if I cannot bear to stay in town.

I will now organize my suitcases and pack my laptops. I carefully apply fresh makeup, groom the ladybits and legs, pull every errant chin hair, check myself for smells. I want to be ready to rut or run.

It has been 30 minutes. Perhaps I can just do my leg drag shuffle over to the Blue Stag Tavern, have a drink by myself and then check out. Berry usually leaves work at 4:30. If he thought to come by on his way home, it might still be too early. Do not dive into despair. Hang on.

Not exactly gracefully executed, but I am at a table at the Blue Stag Tavern. Other vixens might sit at the bar with legs crossed. But there is no way to launch my 200-pound butt up onto a bar stool. Plus, with 27-inch legs, I usually must jump down, which is a dangerous feat as I have no working kneecaps.

I debate what to order. I would like rum and coke or a coffee and Bailey's. If I drive the two hours to Atlanta, I need to be sharp. Thus, Pepper, choose the coffee. On the other hand, if Berry were to come, the coffee might trigger a colonic catastrophe. One which would be sans diaper. One that, even with a diaper and a poop pad, might still make a horrible mess.

If I order a rum and coke – I can get easily stupid drunk as my stomach is empty. After all I did not eat all day because I was afraid…fill in the blank. Still don't get it? If I eat and drink, even marginally, it has to come out. And usually without warning, at the worst time.

If I do drink anything, I might...damn. No matter what, the chances of an accident are over 95.9%. Scientifically proven based on my history.

I am thinking I should just tell the waiter that my companion didn't show so I am going to leave. I reach for my purse and cell phone, and it jiggles. Berry. Can I meet in 5 minutes? Sure.

OMG. I am going to meet Berry!!!! I am so happy. I cannot tell from his text if he is happy. But I will smile and try to get him to laugh. We will just be two strangers and laugh about the Facetime disasters we have had every time we try. Or we can laugh at our naked gardening joke. I can do this. I can be charming. And then in 30 minutes, one drink only, Berry can leave, and I will stay, explaining I am getting a quick dinner, but I know he must get home to his family. Once Berry clears the parking lot, I can try and walk to the front door. I scout the bar for my get-away plan. I see various chairs and coat hooks I can grab to stay upright.

The hotel is less than 100 feet from the bar. And I don't care how I look when I leave alone. Berry will have driven away so no worries. It may crowded at the bar so I won't be seen.

I just will need to get into the hotel room and change because by then I will have hosed my legs and shoes with...you know what.

I admonish myself. Berry is coming. You are on his turf. Do not put on display anything that might hurt his family if they hear about it. Remember your agreement with Berry about discretion. We had text over a month ago on a different matter of intimate sharing, but the rule applies.

Me: *That's our secret please...no matter how famous either of us gets, please.*

Berry: *I hope anything we say can remain our secret*
I trust you with my confidence
And you may do the same

Berry has entered. My gosh he is tall. I give a small beauty queen wave and he joins me. I am trying to read his face. I smile with my Perennial Plum lipstick and white dentures. I open my eyes really big hoping they will dance, delighted to see him. (And not look like a zombie.) I am trying super hard not to be scared. I hope the low bar lights do not emphasize my grey, Diet Coke skin color. I can do this. Thirty minutes max.

Berry sits across from me, rather tight in the booth. Ooh, he is a big dude, and his long knees are so close to mine. He orders a whisky, no ice. I order a rum and coke. Lots of ice. I look at his handsome face. The face I have dreamt of for almost a year. A bit older than the WWF picture. His mustache seems thicker and longer – yes, I have studied his WWF picture to microscopic detail. His eyes are so smiley and amused looking. Ah….

I glance down at his hands. So handsome and furry, my hands are half as long. I lick my lips inadvertently and he notices. You are so young-looking Pepper. I cannot believe you are 62. Your smile is so beautiful.

Ah…I am so yours Berry. Thank you, God. I mean I am sorry God, but Berry is wonderful.

We clink our drinks – chinchin we say and smile. Berry drinks quickly. I sip in measured licks. Must go slow. Must not get stultified. Nor stupid. I lift my gaze from Berry's hands and find him watching my face. I give him my big green eye, black lash blinking look. He smiles. I smile.

This is a strange cognitive dance we are doing…not talking, just like mutually mind reading. I want to advance but am careful. I cannot sense what Berry is thinking. I cannot feel any aura. There are no signals. I almost want to check under the table to see if he brought his tallywacker or if the tallywacker is in charge and his brain is not functioning. Why can't I get a read on this situation?

I blink slowly at Berry and tilt my head and smile. He must be teasing me as he mimics me. I smile with teeth – this is really like watching grass grow, right? Jane Goodall's work observing apes was faster. Good grief.

I lower my eyes to Berry's hands. They are extended on either side of his drink. I take my pointer finger and bring it to the back of his hand.

I look up to see him watching me. I reverently touch his fur in slow, light strokes. Our eyes are locked. I am trying to test his receptiveness. I withdraw slowly. He gently takes his pointer finger and brings it to touch mine. I am melting at the gesture.

Home ET, I say in jest. Home ET, Berry repeats. There is a sudden understanding and Berry flips a $20 on the table and rises. I gather my purse and very carefully try to rise from the booth, attempting grace and dignity. Feeling knees snapping like turtles.

I place my hand on his chest for support. Hopefully, he assumes this is a sexual overture. He turns to leave, and I keep my hand grasping a corner of his shirt. I am wobbling behind him as fast as I can.

In the parking lot he stops. I am 16 inches shorter than he. Jokingly he measures my head against his chest and says – PJ you are just tall enough for this ride. Goody I say in my little kid voice. We walk slowly, at my speed, to the hotel. Not a word.

Once inside my room, Berry goes straight for my lovely view and draws the broken curtains shut. I do a quick bathroom visit, quickly wash all dangerous areas, and come out to see him sitting in my chair of 8 days, legs spread wide. I come to stand in front of him.

I never got my white bag he says.

No sir. I obey orders. I tease back.

Not all orders, he reminds me.

Yes sir. I was naughty.

I may need to spank you.

But sir, I am not wearing any panties.

And I didn't wear any for the next 12 hours.

And I was very, very naughty.

And Berry was naughtier.

Chapter Twelve
THE AFTERLIFE

You can only imagine the Molotov Cocktail of guilt, loss, sadness, remorse, emptiness, loneliness, soullessness that deadened my days. I clung to my faith that God had a Plan in all this disarray. As my nature, I took my angst and studied it on an intellectual level so I could find some containers for sorting all the emotions.

When Dairy Queens no longer could assuage the hunger for peace in my heart, thankfully the clock kept ticking, the days passed. "When someone becomes a memory, the memory becomes a treasure" (Unknown author). I missed Berry beyond heartbreak and the silence in my soul left life without the hope of joy. So too though, with time, I learned to cope. Rose Kennedy wrote, "It has been said, 'time heals all wounds.' I do not agree, the wounds remain. In time, the mind, protecting its sanity, covers them with scar tissue and the pain lessens. But it is never gone."

At two months, I felt I had enough scar tissue preventing my sanity from dropping out of my mind. God seemed to want me to do something for Berry's widow. I couldn't tell if God was leading me to write but I was studying cybersex and infidelity to try and process what I had done. I thought what I had uncovered might be healing. I wrote her a letter.

"Dear Betty,

I am sorry for the loss of your husband. A marriage of 42 years is remarkable. I honor you for this achievement.

I realize anything from me is probably unwelcome. My intention in writing is not to hurt you but perhaps put the events in a perspective that promotes healing.

First and foremost, Berry was never going to leave you, divorce you or hurt you in anyway. You were his love, his mate, the keeper of his past, present and alas, not his future. His relationship with me never came close to the depth of his with you.

Much has been written about "cheaters". And there is no denying Berry cheated. But there is much movement of the line in the sand as to when the cheating started. I have a Catholic perspective but there are secular ones as well.

From what I have researched, Berry entered a type of Conflicted Romantic Infidelity. He had a genuine love for you and a fancy for me. He was not an opportunist cheater that was devoted to his family out of guilt for succumbing to his desire for many some other women. He did not engage with me in obligatory infidelity because of fears of rejection or low self-esteem. Nor was it a romantic infidelity because he was not emotionally attached to you – he was extremely attached to you. And please know deep in your heart, his cheating was not a type of commemorative infidelity where he stayed married for appearances. He was married for life because he loved you.

It appears Berry engaged in a form of micro-cheating. He was lonely and bored at work. He missed your daughter and having family around. He never planned for it to be physical. I am certain he thought it was harmless flirting. Very accidentally it became physical. I know you are probably screaming that men don't just fall into vaginas. Good Point.

And that's where I take responsibility. Some people think of cybersex as just talking about sex online. I considered our online relationship very real. I thought we were both experiencing a real relationship just like an in-person one. I know Berry did not consider it to be morally real – at least not as morally real as if we met in person.

I struggled with the morality or immorality aspect. I am not married. I knew Berry was. With my Catholic upbringing, I believe even an impure thought is a sin. Matthew 5:28 ESV states "But I say to you that everyone who looks at a woman with lustful intent has already committed adultery with her in his heart."

The counterargument believed by many is that cybersex is not infidelity but just an extension to pornography. Akin to reading a smutty book or watching a raunchy movie. Some would argue that cybersex is a means NOT to cheat, just fantasies in a safe environment.

Betty, that is not me. I am not trying to create an image of myself as standing on moral high ground – not at all. I think my relationship with Berry was cheating because it involved so many deceptions. You didn't know about me, it violated your trust in Berry, and Berry may have used resources of time that belonged to you, deepening your marital connection. One thing you must know is that Berry had not wanted to meet initially. He was content living in the parallel world in which he had everything he loved and worked for, and I was just a distraction when he was bored or lonely.

I also wanted Berry to preserve his world, and I absolutely wanted to preserve mine. There was no intention to leave our worlds. No intention for Berry to divorce and collapse his family.

I fervently hope that Berry's infidelity created a more attentive husband. As a marriage therapist, I gave Berry materials, poems, ideas to breathe fresh air into your relationship. I am not trying to justify his infidelity, but to give some positives. He betrayed you. Yes. Did he treat you better in the last few months before his demise? Do you remember seeing

Berry have a new energy, a youthful playfulness? Maybe the 64-year-old Berry was getting re-acquainted with the 22-year Berry? If he had lived, would Berry have achieved a reconnection to the young man that walked down the aisle with you?

Your husband didn't love me romantically. He just liked me whenever he wanted. I was in love with Berry. I thought ours was a real relationship. I am embarrassed to be so naïve. I needed to live the parallel life he provided as my own, was and is, insufferably hard and lonely. Like all people, I just wanted to be understood, known, and loved for not what I could do for others, but for me. I know now that Berry was not this person.

While I am extremely grateful for the lifeline Berry provided during some awful, unbelievable months, I am so sorry for hurting you.

I do not know why God plucked Berry off the earth in such an unseemly manner. I don't know if we die the death we deserve, I think not. I think the method of death is not linked to the life we lived and the blessings we were to others. I hope that you can find the blessings from his life and find some peace with the cause of death.

Pepper"

Should I send this to Betty? I can't hear your answer. Ok. I will wait for at least the 48-hour window I advise my clients. After all I am a professional.

Therapy Session: Pepper

Quick Recap:

Pepper is in her 60's and appears well groomed, if not a bit youthfully dressed. Her hair is dark brown with navy blue highlights. She wears a thick makeup foundation and has heavily lined eyes and false eyelashes that even from a distance appear a bit wonky. There is an unusual size caboose behind her and an overall presentation of a lack of muscle tone.

Pepper is here today to process her concern regarding "excessive weeping".

She asks the readers to "therapize" her. She has no one else because she is a Professional and can usually handle her own stuff.

Session:

Where would you start? Gentle hint: start where your client wants to start.

You: Pepper, what are your goals for therapy today?

Pepper: Thank you for asking, Pepper replies in her professional voice. I am normally a happy person and keep remarkably busy. I have a great family and a great private practice. I hated my grey mom van, so I traded it for a shiny red mom van. I hated the color paint of my house, so I had it painted sunshine yellow with an accent wall of salmon. If something is bothering me, I have the power to improve my own situation!

You might say: that's great but did you have any goals for today?

To which Pepper responds, I have lists of goals every day and I really enjoy crossing them out when accomplished.

You, not showing any impatience, persists: Pepper, what is on your mind today to talk about?

Pepper babbles about all that she must do. She is so happy to do this for someone. She just started volunteering doing something or other. She keeps her house as immaculate as possible despite the number of residents (so many that you as a therapist should have been writing them down).

Then Pepper starts going on about being a Professional, something that seems particularly important to her.

Your mind drifts. You haven't been trained to sit through mindless musings for 50 minutes. You are an action-oriented therapist. Let's get to the meat of the meal and stop decorating the plate, moving this type of food here, no let's place it there, it has to look appetizing and Better Home and Gardens photo ready.

Pepper has wasted almost 40 minutes of her session and it is unclear how this therapy thing works for her. You are numbed by the minutiae. Your brain is ready to fall asleep to the monotone intonations going on and on. How can this droning possibly be beneficial? You consider slapping Pepper's face to bring her back to reality. Or maybe you should slap your own face to wake up.

Five minutes left! You are almost done with your first therapy client! And a tough one at that because she is a fellow Professional! Congratulations!

Stop. Is Pepper crying – she is reaching for a tissue. Are there black smudges under her eyes? Ah shit. Please do not cry, you scream in your brain. There are only 4 minutes left.

Pepper's shoulders heave and she bends completely down towards her feet. Her body is vibrating, and sorrowful sighs are rhythmically expelled. What do you do?

You: Pepper, I apologize but your time is up. I know, Pepper squeaks. Then you hear some odd squirting noise – did she just fart or worse, shit-tart?? Pepper struggles to rise from her chair. She grabs her walker and as she passes you to leave, there is a pronounced urine and feces smell.

Hint for your new therapy practice: allow 30 minutes between Pepper and the next client for airing out and possibly scrubbing the upholstery of your comfy chair.

Chapter Thirteen

I waited 52 hours and emailed my little note to Betty Johnson, widow of Berry Johnson, a man who never belonged to me. Betty responded immediately. No breadcrumbing here.

Betty wrote:

OMG Pepper,

You are insane. Please do not contact me again. You ruined my life in more ways than you can ever imagine.

You murdered my husband. Why aren't you in prison yet?

B

Yes, I did send the letter because I felt it was the professional thing to do. Yes, it was ill-received. Yes, I am so sorry. There are no words. For any of this. At least from me.

I was following Berry's Facebook account. Two days after his death Betty had posted this pithy notice to his 623 friends:

My beloved Berry has passed away. We were married 42 years. We had just celebrated our anniversary on our old stomping grounds, reminiscing about the early days. Berry recited a poem he found for me... he was so romantic. And a good father to Kristi. We are devasted and ask your prayers.

Not surprisingly, Berry's site received 590 responses, some in languages I didn't recognize. All praising Berry the boss, the friend, the relative. When a person dies in their prime there are just so many people to provide accolades. I sure hoped Betty was comforted by all the love.

The town's newspaper initially printed a little blurb that was on the front page.

"Local businessman dies of undetermined causes. An investigation is being conducted. Berry Johnson, age 64, was found dead by police at 1212 Arthur Street. A suspect has been questioned. An autopsy is being conducted. No charges have been filed."

I was – am – still scared. I certainly did not kill Berry, but one never knows how police will view a Yankee, a northerner, "an unpaid sex worker" (yep, Office Jack A Hole asked me if I was one. Yes, sir. Big market for crippled old women...duh.) I do not want to be charged with anything. I have been googling of course and found a YouTube video referenced in the Mirror, 2016. The video was of a prostitute still attached to her client, a pensioner who died during sex. They are both on the stretcher. Well, at least that didn't happen. Like my grandpa would say in his German tongue, "things could ve vurse".

Days later, a tiny follow-up article in the Dublin newspaper put my mind at rest. "Berry Johnson, age 64, died of a heart attack confirmed Dr. Peabody Munson, Medical Examiner. The investigation concluded there had been no foul play."

I should have been relieved by this, but I feared Betty and Berry's family might sue me for his death. Or worse, in Georgia there is an "alienation of affection" lawsuit that spouses can launch. It is an antiquated law that today can net millions (not from me it won't) and is based on revenge and greed. Sorry, Betty. Berry should have cheated with a rich partner with pockets deep enough for you to swim in the cash. Yep, fill your pool up with cash and go swimming. As for me, I have a couple of paper clips and some loose change in my purse. Not worth it.

As for my Minnesota life, no one knew a thing. No one suspected a thing. Wanna know why? Because everyone got fed, had their favorite snacks available, the endless empty toilet tissue and paper towel rollers were constantly filled, the house got cleaned, garbage and recycling went out on time, bills were paid, dinners were served. Holiday family meals were prepared. People got their birthday cards and gifts. No service went unperformed. Robot Pepper is efficient like that.

I think Betty got her wish. I was in prison – certainly of my own making. People depended on me, I provided. I was isolated in the prison of my own mind. Nothing, but occasionally feeling for a heartbeat, reminded me that I was alive.

At night, when all were in bed, I would flip through Berry's texts and the tears would wash the makeup off my face. Black mascara rivers would run into my mouth. All the dick pics seemed so beautiful, so surreal. Then a horrifying thought came to me. Wonder if my cell crashed and I lost my only remnants of Berry?

Ok. How do I preserve them? Should I risk Walmart printing off the dick pics?

No, just use your own printer. They won't be glossy like Walmart's, but I also won't be arrested for trying to print porn. I perked up. Doing something, moving forward was always the answer for me. Just start. Something. Do something. I started a photo album of Berry. Even his Facebook pictures with his family. I printed his resume from LinkedIn. I started that night to type out our bodice ripping texts, the complimentary ones and then just went crazy and started with WWF and vowed to capture the Messenger ones to. I had something to do. I was already feeling a smidge less dead.

Plus, if I were ever charged with a crime or "alienation of affection", the evidence would not be on my cell phone. I know you are thinking there is the Cloud storing the evidence of our lives forever. Well, I don't know about what I don't know, so please don't tell me what I don't want to know.

Month three and I have not cracked the veneer of servitude. No one in Minnesota knows. I wonder if I am safe. I monitor the Dublin newspaper daily, and I check Berry and Betty's Facebook as well as their daughter's. Nothing has been written to cause alarm.

And then it happened. Barney Fife, from the "crime" scene, must have been smoldering a hankering for the hotel clerk who worked the night that Berry was removed in a horizontal position. Apparently, she was incredibly desperate, and Barney was the last single man in Dublin, the moon had turned purple, it snowed in July in Georgia – or whatever ill-fated coincidence befell. They went out and chatted up how they met. How Berry being dead with a Yankee, ha-ha funny.

In full flirt mode, the hotel clerk told how long I had actually been at the hotel before he died. How I was working out of my hotel room and barely ever went out. How she had Googled me, because she thought I might be someone famous because who in the world would spend 11 days in Dublin? And did you know Barney Fife, that she is a marriage therapist?

Weird marriage therapy if the guy dies, heh? Barney Fife immediately radioed in this news to his partner at the station. And his partner, who couldn't get the lurid sex scene out of his mind, told the other guys. And the newspaper's police correspondent thought it was hilarious. And that is how the police file was re-opened. The itemization of the waste baskets and all. And that is how Dublin's newspaper had the only interesting headline since it began in 1904.

"Marriage Therapist found with dead client". Untruth after untruth followed and Berry was resurrected. "The scene of death involved Minnesota therapist, Dr. Pepper James engaging in unknown sex therapy method."

My own heart attack was imminent. I was identified. Named. Located. My life was over. Surprisingly, that voice was of Logical Pepper thinking. How screwed am I when Logical Pepper is thinking this? Where can I run? Who is going to take care of my Littles? What has happened?

I put the Littles in front of the television – watch anything. Super unusual treat for them as I am normally a Nazi on screen time. I went into my office and checked my office for messages, my website, everything. Had anything been violated? Who else knew?

Dublin news reporter Catalina Carolina Smith had left a message for me. Nope. Not talking to her. A 12-year-old voice representing The Atlantic Journal-Constitution Newspaper had also left a message wanting to do a follow up article. Nope. Nothing to report here. Maybe if I just ignore them, they will go away.

That's a good plan.

I checked my cell phone and Betty had Messengered me. "Do something to stop them. A reporter called me for a comment on you. I told her you were a bitch and to leave me alone." Oh no. Please God do not let this get out of control. I am begging you. I have done everything perfectly since it happened. I have served and served. Please have mercy on me. Forgive me. Please.

I wanted to respond to Betty but what do I say? Don't be telling people I am a bitch? It will feed excitement to a bored town. Plus, I am not a bitch. For example, if you must know, the poem Berry read to you on your anniversary, I had sent him so that he could do something special for you. I sent quite a few fun things for Berry to enhance your celebration. I was for your marriage, not against it.

Logical Pepper responded:

Betty, I am sorry that happened to you. I have been contacted too. If we don't respond they will have nothing to write and will hopefully go away. Take care, Pepper

The phone jiggled immediately. It was a text from Betty.

You have no idea what you have done. Everyday something else is happening. I can't deal with any more bad news. It is spinning out of control.

Oh dear. Betty is in distress. I am a professional. So, I write:

Betty,
Sounds super bad. Is there anything I can do?
Pepper

Buzz:

Fuck you. Everything is a mess. And it is your fault.

I am guessing Betty is not able to receive my offer of assistance as it was intended. I am also guessing Betty is in the anger stage of grieving. Yep. She is very angry.

What should I do though? How do I manage the reporters? How can I squelch this superfast before I lose my practice and reputation? Here is a hint if you ever find yourself in a similar situation. Do something.

Because not doing anything didn't work. In the absence of information, the major newspaper in Georgia came up with their own information. Front page, with two paragraphs that followed up in the Life section:

Dr. Pepper James, Marriage and Family Therapist, of Minnesota called 911 on July 10, 2020. Berry Johnson, age 64, had died during their sexual encounter. It is not known if James, age 62, was practicing sex therapy. An investigation into her credentials did not find a license for sex therapy. Betty Johnson, widow, was asked for comment and she told a Dublin reporter James was a bitch. It is unknown the nature of the relationship between Berry Johnson and James. James has not responded to a request for an interview.

The Dublin coroner's report indicated that Johnson died from a heart attack. Researchers from Taft University and the Nepal School of Public Health cite sexual activity nearly triples the risk of having a heart attack. Johnson was a marathon runner, winning trophies in his age category. His Dublin physician did not respond to inquiries on Johnson's health before his death. It is not known if James had knowledge of a heart condition before the encounter.

Continued on page 2 LIFE

Sex and heart attack:

Heart attacks are the major cause of death across the world. The average age for the first heart attack is age 64, Johnson's age. It is not known if James engaged Johnson in any sexual practices which would have increased his risk of a heart attack.

James' therapy practice, STAGES, is located in St. Paul, Minnesota. James is a licensed LMFT with a Ph.D. in Marriage and Family Counseling from Argosy University.

Could it get any worse? I am just reeling over "sex practices". Really? Everyone get their mind out of the gutter. And naming my practice and location? Was that even remotely necessary?

Please God make it stop. I can't lose my practice and support all these people, including the Littles. I am going to have to sell my house and disappear into the northern woods and serve squirrel meat and nonpoisonous berries to the kids.

Logical Pepper, where are you? Google Pepper. Look up something. Stay grounded. Ok. Google – is a heart attack a natural cause of death? Yes, it is unless it happens during a fistfight, then it is a homicide, for example.

So, what we have here is a natural death, at a statistically significant age for a heart attack. There is absolutely no evidence of unusual sex practices. No money transactions ever that would indicate Berry was a client.

The only issue is that I was not his wife. Well, that happens. Roughly 30 to 60% of all married individuals in the United States will engage in adultery at some time in their marriage. Nothing to see here folks. I am not the first or the last to have seduced a cheating man. I googled adultery in the Bible – it is mentioned 52 times, including in the Ten Commandments, all four Gospels, and ten other books of the Bible. I never intended to join The Adultery Club. But it happened. Berry's penis fell into my vagina. (Yes, several times during our one night together.)

Logical Pepper remained with me for a few days. I did not respond to repeated calls from Georgia reporters. It was when the Minnesota Star Tribune reporter called that Wild, Freaked Out Pepper threw Logical

Pepper aside. I wavered between ballistic and suicidal. Not my home paper. Not the paper my clients read. Not in Minnesota, my sanctuary.

Too close. The enemies are coming too close. I kinda missed the part of the Star's message about doing an article on sex after 60...I was so afraid of being linked to Berry's death. So, I didn't respond. Yep, Pepper the Walrus went under water to wait it out. But Walruses only last 30 minutes under water before coming up for air...

Two reporters were at my office when I arrived for the evening clients. The clients looked scared. I was shaken. I had my clients sit in my office while I addressed the reporters. No, I cannot comment. I have no information to give. It is not appropriate to come to my office and impact my clients. This is a breach of confidentiality, and you must leave.

No, I will not meet for an interview. No, I will not be intimidated by your investigation into Berry's death. Ok, I was super intimidated. I gave in and agreed to a meeting. Not interview. I warned the reporters I had nothing to say. One tried to take my picture and I swatted at his cell phone. Get out, I said in my deep, mean scary voice. They left and I entered my office and locked my clients and I in.

When I turned around to apologize to my couple, they were standing to leave. They wanted to know if anyone would see them walking out. I said I would walk ahead and check all hallways and I am so sorry. No charge for today. Please reschedule on the website. Ha! Not fricking likely. Yep. I understand.

I sat in my office and called the remaining clients and rescheduled them. I was wrecked. Emotionally on a razor-sharp edge. Mentally swimming in opaque slime, unable to process anything. Not sure how well I did at the rescheduling, probably messed that up. Jotted a note down to check it later.

Therapy Session: Jesse

Quick Recap:

Jesse is 63-year-old man. Elementary school teacher for 30 years. Married for 15 years to second wife. First marriage was 22 years + 10 years of dating. Concerned with disconnection from his children of 1st marriage.

Jesse is casually dressed in jeans and a plaid shirt. Grooming is adequate. Weight average high. Demonstrates anxiety, fear, nervousness in sessions by tightly clasped hands and foot tapping. He is extremely sensitive – reminder to therapist.

Session:

Idea: Let's be co-therapists with Jesse today.

You begin: Jesse, what brings you here today?

Jesse: My appointment is today, right? Did I get my appointment wrong?

Me: No Jesse. Your appointment is today, and we are glad you are here. Is there anything special you want to talk about today?

Jesse: Was I supposed to bring something special? Did I forget the homework?

You: Jesse, you are okay. We just wonder how we can help you today.

Jesse: Ok. If, you're sure.

Me: Jesse, how has your morning been going so far?

Jesse: Well, I couldn't sleep very well last night because I was worried about today.

You: What worried you about today?

Jesse: Being here.

We wait in silence to see if Jesse will volunteer more. I watch his face because he is so sensitive, he will become anxious if he doesn't receive positive reinforcement pretty quick. Nothing…45 seconds. Jesse's eyes are darting between you and myself… I speak, breaking the silence.

Me: Me too Jesse! I always get a bit anxious before each session starts. Is anxious the right word or how do you feel?

Jesse: Not sure. More worried.

Me: Tell us more about worried please.

Jesse: I'm not sure what you want me to say.

You: You can say anything.

Jesse: Well, now I don't know what and you probably think I'm dumb.

Me: Not dumb. This is a judge free zone. Let's do what you want to do. No worrying about dumb, making a mistake, spilling your Diet Coke... it all happens here so no reason to be worried.

Hint: it has been almost 15 minutes of this. Jesse will spend nearly the whole 50-minute session going around and around. At every session, I have recommended he see a physician because the word anxiety is screaming at me. Poor guy seems almost catatonic he is so afraid of everything. Could be high blood pressure or other issues. At any rate, a whole-body physical seems like the place to begin. But guess what? He is afraid to make an appointment. I have even offered to have him call during our session, but he has declined. Frankly, if he made the appointment, who is to say he will get there?

If I am a safe place for him to spin for 50 minutes, I would prefer he keeps coming in until he is ready. As I conclude today's appointment, I use my Readiness Ruler. He rather enjoys this tool.

Me: Jesse, may I ask you a question?

Jesse: Okay (but enunciated okaaaaaaaaaaaaaaaay...).

Me: On a scale of 0 to 10, what number would you rate your interest in making an appointment with your doctor for a physical? 0 is no interest and 10 is I will make it right now in front of you Dr. Pepper.

Jesse: I think about a 3.

Me: Thank you Jesse. I am curious why today you are a 3 and not a 2?

Jesse: Well, a 2 is almost a 0. And my brother and sister now have diabetes, so I should probably check on that.

Me: Oh my. Diabetes. That's not good. Diabetes can be serious. What would it take for you to be a 4?

Jesse: I don't know. Maybe if I talked to my mom about diabetes in the family?

Me: Interesting. I can see that might change things. Can that be your homework for the week? To call your mom and discuss the family history of diabetes?

Jesse: Sure.

Are you interested in more information?

1. Motivational Interviewing is a counseling approach developed by Miller and Rollnick. The Readiness Ruler is a tool and conversational method that allows you to understand if making a change is important to your client or the person you are using it with. Provides a gauge on their willingness to change and commitment to acting on their decision.

   This is a good tool if you are a supervisor, a parent, a partner, a roommate. For example:

   Gus, on a scale of 0 to 10, how ready are you to take out the garbage?

   Gus says 5.

   Well Gus, what would it take to get from 5 to 7?

   Gus: another beer.

   See how much you can learn from the Readiness Ruler?

   If Gus is a 5 it helps you decide your level of acceptance of this. Do you take out the garbage yourself or give Gus a chance for his motivation to increase?

   Note how you have not nagged Gus? You are just gathering information.

Chapter Fourteen

How am I going to meet the reporters tomorrow? I need my eyelash extensions redone as they are twisting up on me. My hair needs root maintenance. I can't be seen, much less photographed looking like an arrest mugshot. First impressions are so important. I am going to fail right away from my utterance of word one. Foot inserted in mouth, like it was Berry's dick. Oh no...Berry's dick. And the tears started flowing.

I miss Berry's beautiful dick pics. I'm never going to get a dick pic from Berry again. I start wailing...dick pics...oh Berry. I can't do this. I can't live. Robot Pepper had done her best all these months. Pepper-the-person was alive and horribly sad and had come out of hiding. Exposed. Vulnerable. Alone.

It never was about the hair and eyelashes. You knew that. It was about loss. Loss of Berry. Loss of my clients. Loss of my privacy. From now on I would be on display for criticism, rejection, ridicule, reprisal and my family learning about their mother, sister, daughter and her secret, parallel universe.

Ok God. I have my cross. I am picking it up. I will be vilified when I just wanted to be loved. Like Jesus. He just wanted to show the world how to love. Ok, He was sinless, and I am an uber sinner. But I still am going to have to carry my cross to the crucifixion of my soul.

I went home, found 10+ half eaten meals, 13 snack wrappers scattered from the back door to the kitchen. Clean laundry was mounted on my recliner, unfolded, and unsorted. The dog had not been fed and gave me the mournful eye look. Pots and pans indicating a Thanksgiving Day feast were all over the kitchen. Garbage and recycling bins were spilling over. Headless Barbie dolls were scattered amidst Lego's. Thanks, family, for picking up. The maid has arrived. The magic begins.

I worked until about 2 am straightening up and running loads of laundry. Couldn't sleep anyway. Was frenetic with fright. When the mystical process of cleaning up was completed, I showered and dressed for my "meeting". I sat at 3:47 am clutching my Berry photo album and praying that I would be delivered from the executioner.

I made the Littles their breakfast trays at 4:12 am and put them into the fridge. I played WWF until 5:33 am. I walked the dog and fed her breakfast. Robot Pepper had arrived for duty. When the time came to drive to the "meeting", I was methodical, quiet. My favorite mantra, God has the Plan, was in an endless loop in my brain. God is in control. God wants me to prosper – remember? Faith, hope, love. God is with you.

I met two young female reporters. They were surprisingly deferential. I wonder if they saw me as scary old. Or maybe because I am a Professional. Whatever their issue, I am intimidated by them.

The questions are basic. Age. Profession. Education. How long have I lived in Minnesota? Little tougher, do I have an opinion on the viability of marriages? What are my thoughts on the concept of soulmates, one special person for everyone? What role do I see marriages play in society's fabric?

What are my thoughts on infidelity? Yep. Here we go. I got through the T-ball stage of the game with light plastic balls. Now we're going for Fast Ball. Please God do not let Aroldis Chapman, who pitched a 105.1 mph ball, be disguised as a reporter today. I deferred the reporters to the work of Esther Perel, a leading authority on infidelity.

How common is it to be sexually active after age 50? Age 60? I replied that Google is my friend on statistics, but I have not experienced anyone these ages lacking in desire or ability. I mentioned that nursing homes have stories to tell of wandering seniors doing the mattress mambo at night. The reporters giggled. Yep. I laughed with them.

In my normal fashion of talking too much, I told the story of when I was an intern for a small optical shop. I was 16 years old and supposed to learn to adjust glasses frames, read lens powers with a lensometer, learn to choose stylish frames to fit faces and in general do – SOMETHING CONSTRUCTIVE – with my summer. Here is the only thing I remember.

Every faucet has a way to be turned on.

What??? The almost 70-year-old perverted shop owner had a thing for my mother. He told me that he was a man that knew how to turn on even the hardest faucets. Yes. This happened. I can't remember most anything these days but his ugly face of drooping jowls and bulbous nose (alcoholic?) sneering this line at me, that I remember clearly.

The "girls" were delighted by my candor. Yep. I can be full of candor. Full of something, that is for sure. Next question, how do you meet men after age 50?

Ok. Were they playing me? Online sites, E-Harmony, Catholic Singles, bars, grocery stores, churches? Pretty much the same as at their age. What? They expected me to reveal the seedy side of a Bingo Hall? Cruising Target picking up guys in line as we both try to hide the disposable underwear in our carts? Maybe at Dentures-R-Us? Are we done here?

Nope. Here it was. The question I had hoped to avoid. How did you meet Berry? Tell us how you went from a chat box to flying to Georgia to meet him. We are extremely interested, so where do you want to start?

Nowhere. Thank you. I do not want to start. I do not want to start and finish with I am lucky to be alive because Berry died on top of me and nearly crushed me. I am not here for your enjoyment. Interview over.

But it turns out it wasn't over. Like an infectious disease, the Associated Press News (APS) picked up the young ladies' story. The picture they took was fairly flattering, I looked about 45 years old. (Thank you, God.) So maybe my picture sold the story? (Always about appearances, right?).

Parade Magazine called to do a feature article on Geriatric Sex. What? How did I become a spokesperson for geriatric sex? I was still a 13-year-old at heart. And by God, I certainly didn't want to look geriatric. Although, I am not quite sure what geriatric looks like. Must google geriatric appearances.

I had to do a lot of research before the Parade interview. Had notecards of facts, had written quotes in the palms of my hands. And up my short skirt, I had written in black thin tipped marker other pithy bits of information. I may not have a memory anymore, but I can come prepared.

The reporter for Parade wanted me to define "geriatric". Good thing I had googled the definition. I had been shocked to learn that geriatric started at age 65. How is that possible? Berry was 64 and one of the most athletic lovers (pounded me like a butcher tenderizing a sirloin), his sex drive was so much stronger than my memories of my 18-year-old, Chevy Malibu days, and he was more creative than the Kama Sutra.

Oh, excuse me, back to providing the officially googled version of "geriatric".

I started to provide it, Robot Pepper intoning "Geriatric is a term relating to old people, particular regarding their medical needs. Age 65 is the age often used but people do not need geriatric medical expertise until the 70's usually."

I am sorry, I told the reporters. This is absolute rubbish. There is no way on earth I will be geriatric at age 65. I totally doubt it at 70. I have career goals that bring me to 80. Travel goals into my late 80's. I intend to be a homeowner and live independently until I am 100. At 100, I will consider being geriatric. Meanwhile, I am looking for my life partner #3 who will be with me from say ages 65 to 85. At which time, according to statistics he will die. However, I reject that. We will have so much fun and take such good care of each other, we may beat the statistics.

I may use a walker and cane now. But science may figure out how to solve these problems. There are motorized wheelchairs, handicapped vans. I hope that Ford Mustangs come out in a wheelchair model. I loved my 1975 Mustang II and would like to own another Mustang.

Well, the reporters are sitting there nodding like – you, Dr. James, are a doddering fool. You are old. Just give it up. You are wasting social security money that we will need. What a drain on society. I can read minds and I am certain that is what they were thinking.

I could possibly have been wrong. My militant manner on opposing being called geriatric hit a chord with their readership. AARP asked for an interview. Suddenly, the absurd notion that people over 60 could be horny and possibly getting more action than 20-year-olds, became in vogue. And because I was genetically blessed with moderately younger looks, my picture got out there. A lot.

At any rate, my practice had recovered from the notoriety of my canoodling a married man. I even developed a bit of a specialty in infidelity as I had been on both sides and had an appreciation for the complexities and nuances. I raised my rates because I could see much fewer clients what with all the interviews, and copious googling I had to do to appear sharp and current.

I hired a tutor for the Littles as we were starting to travel a bit for speaking engagements and my primary responsibility was to meet their needs first. I left the house in the least capable hands of my adult children. I hired a weekly cleaning crew, lawn maintenance team, pool man, snow removal service, a part time secretary and a publicist. The laundry continued to be a problem, but I was confidant, that they could figure it out. And since they were decades over 10 years old, they might as well learn to cook and grocery shop for themselves. It was an outstanding opportunity to grow up.

I carried my Berry photo album less frequently. When I needed a fix, I had a single dick pic folded in my wallet. I prayed all day, every day "God has the plan". Some days I wasn't sure I could do what He was asking of me. I am not a public speaker. I don't think I give "good couch" for talk shows. I get so damn lonely I need to be incredibly careful not to think strangers are friends. Staff are not friends. I had no friends I could trust. Everyone wanted something from me, not a situation I was unfamiliar with. Felt like home.

My number one concern, now that I was exposed to the scary world, was my propensity to attract narcissists like sharks to urine. (I know people think sharks are attracted to blood but google says sharks are more attracted to unusual fluids like urine.) I have lots of urine, so the metaphor works. At any rate, I have zero radar on narcissists.

Narcissists zoomed in. All smart, skilled at lying, usually intelligent. Oh baby, come here! I am a Sapiosexual. (*Sapiosexual is a person who finds intelligence in others sexually attractive or arousing. Berry said he was definitely a Sapiosexual!) and smart people are a turn on. If the man is also physically attractive, granted anyone less attractive than Berry still meets a high bar, and oozes a bit of desirableness, I'll pay attention. If the narcissist can effectively portray themselves as empathic and caring, the long-lost tomb of Pepper's vagina starts squeaking open. A few more attributes like successful and power yielding and I am primed. Or use to be primed. Thank God I am not young and still have a lifetime of heartache ahead of me.

I would rather be alone, tightly clenching my financial portfolio, than ever, ever be abused again and robbed. See? Mistrustful of myself around men. Been there, done it several times multiplied by several more, done now for good. Speaking of sharks, even my service providers were circling the unusual fluid waters.

My wonderful beautician of 13- years, was an entrepreneur with product lines to promote. The shampoos and conditioners and wet slicky stuff was free with the caveat I had to promise I would promote her. My eyelash queen gave me Cleopatra thick, glamour lashes and stopped trying to tell me to go with a "natural" look. I am 62+ years old. Why would I want to look natural ladies?

Can you mention my cupcake business? Tell 'em you got your nails done at Naughty Nancy's Nails (formerly Nancy's Nails but adding "Naughty" brought in more business). Can you slip it out that you like staying at Holiday Haven's Hotels? (Excuse me, it was more like Harrowing Hell Hotel…why did a Little find an old toy in his bunkbed? Gross.) Free tattoo of Berry's face if you say where you got it done?

Yep. Mercenaries. Not all of them though. I was on a late-night talk show chatting it up about the difficulties of sex after a broken hip when the conversation turned abruptly to sin-after-sixty. Mm…my antennae detected danger. I was asked about my thoughts on sinning.

Well, sinning is bad. Sinning is turning away from God. God is in control. As people God has placed purposelessly on this planet, we have a mission. To love and to serve. If we are sinning, we are not working our mission. God has a plan for each of us. God's plan is to help us prosper and not to harm us. I personally keep trying to follow God's plan. My mantra is "God has the plan".

The audience clapped long and hard. I looked at the host and said maybe we should all get that tattooed on our hand, so we remember it all day long. The host said, how about bracelets like the once popular WWJD ones. The audience clapped.

The next day I received several emails proposing I endorse their bracelets. They were designing the full sentence God Has the Plan on a variety of materials from rubber bracelets to silver, gold and pewter. I responded to each manufacturer that I would not provide an endorsement unless all profits went to some charity. Dead silence.

No matter. If the bracelets were sold and people wore them, all good. God would become a part of their day. If no one wanted to donate to charity, this feat alone was worth all the tragedy and strife. But if just one manufacturer would donate, I wanted it to go the National Alliance for

Mental Illness. The work they do is so critical for the well-being of everyone, whether suffering, surviving, impacted directly or indirectly.

One huge United States manufacturer stepped up. Theirs were the rubber ones that would be affordable for nearly everyone. Something quite good happened out of something unbelievably bad. Thank you, God, for trusting me with such a big project. They were onboard with donating 35% of the profits to my charity and assuring me they paid a living wage to employees with benefits.

Another weird twist also happened, and I imagine you will be amused. You recall my unique lower body problems? Well, Kimberly-Clark flew me to their design headquarters in Chicago's Loop. Fancy building, newly remodeled. Ooh la-la! I was hosted regally while they picked my brain and listened to an actual avid user of women's disposable underwear. I sat at a gorgeous glass table, in a special black chair they scrambled to find. The matching chrome/glass chair I had been offered was uncomfortable on my spine and I couldn't touch the floor because it was designed for Berry's height. The old black rolling chair with the sunken seat was 15 inches from the floor and it worked. Ah, it felt just right, ala Goldilocks. Although, I looked like a 5-year-old in the Board Room with everyone on their perches.

I had prepared myself for the meeting on disposables by drinking a liter of Diet Coke. I had googled fabrics that absorbed liquid. I researched the average sizes of women's butts standing versus sitting. I also wanted to contribute to the frustratingly negative sizing labels. I even had comments to make about trying to rip into their packaging with arthritic fingers. Like couldn't they have a serrated area – almost like a tissue box to open the packaging. I had suggestions for the models on the packages. The package of the XL Depends products had a chubby model who apparently didn't own a properly fitting brassier. Go google it! Why is her left boob facing California and the right facing New York? Why are there 11 states between them?

The liter of Diet Coke did its job. I started urinating without warning, then could not stop (no Kegel Muscles at all). I sat attentively. When I was sure I was finished, I stood. I announced to the 10 designers, marketers, and researchers that I had to go to the ladies' room, and by the way, watch my butt. This is what a liter of Diet Coke looks like, and this pronounced waddle is what happens when the disposable is completely soaked. I stood up sans walker and shuffled across the room. My short pencil skirt made of polyester/rayon/nylon/spandex bulged in front and back. The pad nearly peeking from the bottom of the skirt.

Go ahead and laugh. I amply made my point. I made it to the bathroom 2 blocks away from the conference room and realized I had not brought a spare disposable. I shed the big wet pillow – noting that the women's individual stall does not have a receptable big enough for a loaded disposable undie. I went to find a receptionist desk to ask if there were any disposable undies in the building. No, there were not. In the entire Kimberly-Clark building, the manufacturer of all things disposable, there was not a Depends or Silhouette. I was desperate. I would have taken a used sample or demo. All the 30-something year olds that worked there had no idea why it was a problem to have a zillion dollar building and not have any of the product they manufacture, available.

Shortly after my Chicago debut, I began receiving package after package of promo disposables. I liked all the free stuff! I rated them on my own rating scale and emailed my comments. Most were just revisions of the same pillow versus menstrual pad. Product fails. Until one day I received a sporty black model. Now we're feeling our youth yet able to fill our pants!

I reluctantly allowed my enormously dimpled, un-photoshopped butt and legs to be photographed in an advertising campaign for a brand of disposable underwear, made with my specifications. "Woman Enough" was the new brand name. The pad was of an absorbent material used to soak up oil in the ocean. It was quite thin and grew with need. The panty itself was seamless on the legs. The waist was elastic for most girths. The butt itself was tractor wide type generous because I hated having to keep grabbing the narrow butt fabric to cover the other cheek. I posed with a modest black chiffon blouse and push-up bra and my new black "womanly" sized disposables. I had requested that S/M/L/XL be banished in favor of Petite/Mature/Lovingly/Womanly.

Fellow disposable wearing women like me – you are welcome. "Win today, and we walk together forever" proud and confident, dry, and comfortable. Original quote from Fred Shero, 1974, before game six of the Stanley Cup Finals, maligned for my purposes.

I want to share the last perk of my 15 minutes of fame with the Diet Coke addicts. All you water drinkers just skip the following couple of paragraphs. If you prefer Diet Coke's competitor, just hush. For I, Dr. Pepper James, received a year's supply of Diet Coke. Just for always drinking one during my interviews. Now granted, a life's supply is a relative term. I am sure Coca Cola thought sending me 144 16-ounce bottles constituted a year's supply. But they sorely underestimated what a fan I was. I was a fan about 15 times the 144.

Not to mention the household of Diet Coke thieves I had to contend with. Thanks for the 144 bottles but they were gone before the week's end. I welcome any additional amount you deem appropriate as I have at least two in my gigantic purse at all times, one bottle is always open in my hands and several partial bottles arranged around me. TIP: if you open a Diet Coke bottle, drink a couple of tablespoons worth, tighten the cap – no one steals it!

I am also offering my services for a Diet Coke commercial of people in their 60's, sober, and enjoying life because their addiction to Diet Coke is accepted in society! No need to exchange money – just send a weekly pallet of Diet Coke!

Chapter Fifteen

Now the anniversary of Berry's death was a couple of weeks away. I was hoping for a low key, media-less day. Just me and the Littles at a waterpark in Wisconsin. The three of us, just being two kids and a wobbly grandma on the waterslides.

Betty had never left my thoughts and prayers. What, pray tell, would you be feeling if your dead husband's lover was joking it up amidst celebrities? Or you opened up your mailbox to her face on the cover of AARP magazine? You couldn't watch the late show on TV without her plopped on the couch, hogging two cushions. Or having her pithy quotes plastered all over? How about your dead husband's lover's dimpled ass printed on disposable underwear packages, available in fine stores such as Walmart and Target and online through Amazon? And those damn bracelets on everyone's wrists. Yep. Did I say I was sorry enough? Probably not.

I was contemplating Messenger to contact her. There had been no updates to her Facebook or her daughter's the entire year. Berry's condolence messages ceased coming a few months back. What did God think about reaching out?

Do it. Clearly spoken. What??? How do I hear God so clearly? I hear God in many ways. Today while I was praying and asking God about Betty, I went to my wallet. I was strongly desiring to see Berry's Rubenesque Staff of Life. (I know. How is this the least bit religious?) Reading your thoughts further, I know, why would I want God to know I carried Berry's dick pic in my wallet? Believe me, nothing escapes God. God knows everything.

I went to pull out my worn out, multi folded picture of Berry's you-know. It tore in my hands. The sign. God's way of talking to me. That would mean, yes Pepper. Text her.

Hi Betty,

How has life been? I hope you are doing ok.

On a scale of 0 to 10, with 0 being not at all and 10 being, yes for certain: how interested are you in having a conversation with me?

You are always in my thoughts and prayers.

Pepper

Twinkly star music immediately followed (I had upgraded my cell phone). Betty responded:

0 if you just want to talk
0 if you treat me like a client
5 if you have any idea what Berry's password for his laptop might be
6 if you know where he kept his desk and file cabinet keys
8 if you know who Mari Moline is

Wow. So, this is a positive! I texted her back that although I have no knowledge of any of those things, I will think about it. I could google Mari Moline a bit for you.

I waited for Betty to respond. Something started bugging me about the password. I am certain Betty would have tried birthdates, family names, pet names, street name, restaurant names. But what about places where they had traveled? His favorite TV show or author? How about a Scrabble word that he liked to play? (DHOTI – a real word! A garment worn by male Hindus). Or how about his name for his "junk"? He liked to call his stuff "manhood".

I texted Betty my top choices for password. Manhood or Manhood64 or Manhood1955. Just a wild guess.

I didn't hear from Betty for 8 days. Manhood64 had gotten her into his laptop and there she found another, yes ANOTHER, parallel universe. A universe where Berry and a Mari sent a family Christmas card from Haiti. What?

It seems Mari Moline is not just a co-worker from one of his former employments. She is the mother to 3 daughters. And good ole Berry was the biological father to all. And the thousands of pictures of the girls with Berry bore an uncanny resemblance to Betty's daughter with Berry. Absolutely beautiful brown skinned girls with black fringed chocolate brown eyes. And tall, lithe figures.

Betty sent a scan of one picture – good job Betty. The pretty little things, pictured climbing on their handsome father, appeared to be maybe 7, 9 and 11 years old. Bit hard to tell because Berry was a giant and his daughters were probably above average heights. I was trying to read the innocence of their faces to judge how old they were. As the youngest had a purer joy and less teeth in her smile, that one was easy. Six years old if in the 100th percentile for height. Seven if in the 80th or lower. The older one still looked sweet, without the burden of pain the world had in store for her. And I figured Berry's penis fell into Mari's vagina about two years apart, making the middle one, nine years old.

Berry had an entire existence in Haiti that Betty knew nothing about. Betty knew that Berry always travelled for his various positions. He had always liked being on the road for 80% of the work week. She had no idea he was traveling to Haiti so often that he could own a house, raise a family and be a contributing member of Haiti's elite Delmas community.

Betty saw pictures of his home in Haiti – a 5-bedroom, 4 bath home with an additional home for 5 staff. He had a 4-car garage. The evidence of his life in Haiti, photos and address was within a file marked Moses on the Mount on Berry's desktop. Moses, heh? How Episcopalian of you.

Mari Moline looked to be about 42 years old, about 5'6 (estimated from a picture of her with Berry). In the picture, she weighed in around 140 pounds, very tan, athletic looking. Decently good looking if you think brunette, tan, toned arms and legs, and normal features on a face constitutes good looking. She was gazing up at Berry, her hand resting on his flat stomach. Gag me.

I googled the house address – in Haiti, where Haitians make about $450.00 a year in US currency. The house was in the $200,000 range. Quite, quite nice there Berry. The house was located in the community of Delmas, a rich commune in the Port-au-Prince Arrondissement. So, with say, 5 servants at $450.00 a year Berry was only shelling out $2250.00 to have his honey's every need provided and the household well maintained in his absence. Unfreaking believable.

Betty was ready to talk. And talk. And talk. I agreed to arrange childcare for the Littles and fly down. I wanted to see the files myself. Plus, Betty had clearly never paid any bills during their marriage, and she was clueless about what bank accounts they had, whether they were still even open. I frankly can't imagine how she stayed solvent this past year with so little financial acumen.

Betty explained that until she could access Berry's laptop that she had had no idea where to begin. The Plan was that she would try to organize bank accounts, where Berry's 401K's from his various employments might be, and if she could find a Will online. Although, there was so much forensic work to do, I did not want to overwhelm her.

I could not wait to see Mari Moline's response on Facebook to Berry's death. That she was a Facebook friend, didn't that translate to she knew he had another family? Mm…so you know a man is married and has a wife and daughter. But you start a relationship (It happens. Men's penises fall into vaginas apparently more often that I thought.). You get pregnant because you wanted to, or it was an oops? And then you get pregnant two more times because you can't figure out birth control or because you are in a committed relationship and want a family? With a married man?

Help me out. What? Where is the moral compass here? Mm... Berry? Mr. I-fantasize-about-it, but morally I can't think about it seriously? This is all very confusing. Berry.

Meri Moline, friend among over 600 friends of Berry's on Facebook, had written:

Betty and Kristi, so sorry to hear this.

Now, I want to extend grace. Wouldn't the mother of Berry's 3 other daughters be grieving and in shock? Who is her support system since she existed in a parallel universe? The staff? The community Berry volunteered with? Parents from their daughters' school? Haitian friends they barbequed with? People on the other side of the world who loved Berry, trusted him, and were blessed by his wonderful personality?

My fingers were flying over Google. I needed everything on Mari Moline. Her Facebook had zero pictures with Berry in them. Strange. Her Facebook was set up almost like a LinkedIn, job seeking, austere account. Facebook did not mention the daughters.

It occurred to me Mari might have a personal Facebook under some version of her name. I opened up each of her Facebook friends to see if anyone could lead me to a real glimpse. Nothing. No family connections, no friends. No amount of drilling down into Facebook provided any clues.

I paid $14.99 for a public search on Mari Moline. No traffic tickets. No jail time. No relatives. Clearly, I didn't have enough information to do a good search. Hate when that happens. Makes snooping so difficult. Whine, whine, whine.

I cannot get to Dublin fast enough. Sorry Betty, but I am self-motivated here. I have spent my life not feeling special and then there was this flash of potential. Now we are finding that neither of us were special enough for Berry. I need to know more.

I packed with urgency. I was researching for a book on sex after 50. I was sick of it being coined "geriatric sex". For goodness' sake. Geriatric connotes fragile elderly. Fifty, sixty and seventy are way too young to be referred to as geriatric. I was going to change the world's image of us and then the lexicon.

After an uneventful flight and rental car registration, I was going to rip into the two-hour drive. I hadn't consider making a hotel reservation. There were plenty of chains. Or maybe I would sleep in Berry's bed at his house, as I assumed, they hadn't shared a bedroom in years. (Oh. Don't be all shocked. Statistics state that 30-40% of couples do not sleep in the same bed. Believe me, my snore is close to 92 decibels, which is like having a diesel truck revving its engine by your eardrum. You want me not only in my own bed but possibly down the street.)

If I were to sleep in Berry's bed, would it still smell like Berry? Have his fur strands on the sheets? Would I start crying like I am now just writing this? What is wrong with me? As the truth of his duplicity is revealed, I am still mourning over the loss. Come on. Pull it together.

Seriously. Stop. Crying. You are in Atlanta's traffic quagmire and need to focus. Tears are falling so fast, and I have no tissues. Hence, they are free falling. The car will soon start filling with water and I will drown by my own means. Adios Pepper. Oh no. That was Berry's salutation. Oh God help me. I am absolutely devastated. Where can I pull over, open my suitcase, and grab some clothes to cry into?

Now that is enough Real Pepper. Logical Pepper here, reporting for mop up duty again. AGAIN. Let's make a list Pepper. Lists cheer you up. Focus.

Do you think Betty has filed for Berry's Social Security Survivor Benefit and death benefit? The death benefit is about $253 so not much. But would offset the costs of groceries or a utility bill or a locksmith if we can't break into his desk drawers and file cabinet. Berry's social security is probably over $2000 a month since he held lofty executive positions. That should help Betty float.

Did Betty file for Berry's life insurance? If he went cheap, it should be at least one year's income. Another boost for Betty. Any chance Berry went for like a million or two million whole life policy? Let's pray so. The way Betty sounds she may need live-in help or be in a more supportive living space.

Put on list to check if Betty has called a realtor yet to get the property evaluated. I wonder if a person needs to find the title before calling. Put that on the list.

How bad is the yard and the pool if it's just been Betty to care for the plantation and the 5 acres? May need to look up lawn and pool services to prep before even having the realtor come. How about interior Painting? Paint the neutral colors right away?

I am so much calmer. I swear to you – if you are nearly immobilized by sadness or depression, try making lists of things to get done. Really focuses and distracts. When you are safe to sit in your pain (I do not recommend when driving in traffic, waiting rooms of banks or auto repair sites), then go ahead and vent, and cry, flushing it all out.

At last, I am on the narrow dirt driveway, to the compound I had once joked was a Unabomber's dream. Last year I spent my days in Dublin, watching, and stalking the driveway. Last year, I was restraining myself from sneaking down the driveway with the rental car. This time, I am welcome, relatively speaking.

I notice the uncut grass. Berry used a riding lawn mower every Wednesday to mow. We had a joke that he should mow naked, and I would sit in a lawn chair watching him, sipping mojitos. He said I could sit on his lap and mow with him. Oh no. Stop. Stop. Mustn't be crying when I meet Betty. Oh F. Too late. Watershed cometh.

Lawn mowing never was so sexy:

Me: *Can I steer the big lawn tank when you mow? Pretty please?*

Berry: *You can sit in my lap and yes, I'll let you steer, if you're a good girl*

Me: *I promise I'll be super good. Maybe we could bring a picnic blanket, bottle of chilled Moscato and find some remote spot for a little well-deserved reward?*

Berry: *Finding that remote spot would be fun*
Especially with you on your best behavior

Me: *Out of curiosity, what does good behavior look like?*

Berry: *You've got to be careful when steering that big mower*
Can't run over logs
And you've got to handle shift level carefully or it will break

Me: *The log I care about, I'll be sitting on*
I can drive a stick, does that help?

Berry: *LOL*
Experience in handling the stick gives you a leg up

Me: *Great. I still can do 2 legs up too!*

Berry: *That might make it a little harder, we'll have to see*

Me: *Should I get my short skirt on for the mower?*

Berry: *The short skirt question left me speechless. I'm thinking the mowing is going to take a good long time. Skirt would definitely be preferred.*

Betty has come onto their log cabin porch. She is much grayer than the old Facebook pictures. Her shoulders are rounded in. She has a faded peach colored, flowered sweatshirt top and sweatpants on. With her are two older looking, tired gray whiskered dogs. I immediately wonder if the third one passed as Berry thought he might. Oh God. Loss. Loss. Loss.

Betty's hair, shown in last year's pictures as a blondish red, was now light brown and streaked with grey strands. She was now Minnesota-white, pale, as though the winter of her discontent had faded her tan. She was taller than the 5'6 I had imagined. More like 5'8 to 5'10?

She was wearing tennis shoes that could possibly have been white but showed years of gardening dirt, dust, painting and staining on them.

I assume by her apple shape – large bosom and slender legs – she might have been athletic. Berry had once asked if I played tennis. (He had no idea of how unlikely that was!) And there had been Facebook pictures of a weekend trip where Berry and family had hiked. Again, I assumed she hiked with Berry and her daughter.

The contrasts between Betty and I continued. Her eyes were puffy and swollen and showed symptoms of some disease I couldn't quite discern. Mine are not puffy but red-rimmed from too much eyelash growth serum. Plus, I had nearly black half-moons under my eyes from my overly applied mascara. Although some darkness was from the lashes smudging, some was from constant insomnia and perhaps some darkness attributed to dehydration from 2 liters of Diet Coke a day.

I had kinda put together there may have been an infertility issue because their daughter was born 12 years after they married. Was there any correlation with her protruding eyes and wonky hormones? Wish I had a brain that remembered things…at any rate I had assumed that she was probably depressed and anxious as a baseline. Frankly (and when you hear the word "frankly" before anything, brace yourself) if I looked like Betty, and Berry looked like he did, I would be a wreck, and very clingy and miserable.

There is no fight in Betty. She doesn't really want to shake my hand and gives me a limp flipper. Ok. I know she has some disease. Berry didn't specify what, but I will be gracious and assume the limp was as welcoming as she can be.

I am aware that I am lively and energetic, despite my cane. I try to tone down the voice to match her softness. There is nothing I can do now about the black and navy-blue hair or my caterpillar like eye liner and three-inch-long fake eyelashes. Underneath all that vanity is a real person.

There is no offer of sweet tea. Zero Southern hospitality. We go straight to Berry's office. A visual nightmare of papers once stacked and spilled everywhere. Betty shows me the locked desk drawers. No key, heh? My first thought is that it must be taped under the desk. Uh. Does that mean I have to get on my knees to look? I really can't get up if I even can crack the knees to get down. Yep. Betty is staring at me.

I do a quasi-flop on the floor which is a way of not bending the knees but placing a lot of pressure on my hands to hold me while I fall. I fell a bit too far from the desk. Dang. I do an army crawl closer. Knees are useless. Under the desk is So Much DUST, DANDER, DEAD BUG CARCASSES. There are petrified 1- year old Cheetos half eaten. Gross. I am in a Professional's outfit for flying. I am not dressed to dust this filth. Ugh.

Believe it or not, the sight of a Cheeto that Berry may have had in his mouth is not filling me with desire. Nor am I gushing tears out of every portal. This is disgusting.

Nevertheless, I must find the keys. Wish I had gloves, but I do not. Please skin protect me from spiders, webs, and Southern Georgia mystery bugs. I carefully wipe back and force under the bottom side drawer. Nothing. Along the inner sides I feel for tape scum. I shine my cell light to see if there is a mystery pocket anywhere. Now I boost myself directly under the long main center drawer. It should be here.

I am going so slow. I never want to be doing this again. I need a shower immediately. I poke into every little ledge and indent. Quite a bit of crumbs sprinkling into my hair. Please do not be broken spider legs God. There is not a key. I try to slide the drawer manually to see if anything catches underneath or drops. Nothing like a key falling but chunks of petrified black salsa drop down. The latter would make sense given the sloppy tortilla chip eating that must have been going on.

I am now on the left side set of drawers. These drawers go to the floor and have indented the carpet. I think we need to tip the desk over to see if the key is under this set of drawers. After all, what looks like a 60-70-pound oak desk that might give Betty and I, the butter queens, trouble, would be nothing for the man who fantasized about lifting me up and porking me against the wall.

Betty agrees and places her little white hands to push it up. Good god. Not yet Betty. #1 I am underneath. #2 you don't look like you could push a pencil. #3 I need about 15 minutes to get up from the floor. I am looking desperately for something solid to cling to and pray my spine allows me to pull from an angle. And of course, there is the filth factor. What is the least dusty, moldy thing I can touch for support? Gross! This room is an entire turn off.

I am checking the shelves of an assumable built-in cabinet behind Berry's desk chair. Sturdy enough to support 200 pounds leaning on it? Lots of books. Lots of obscure titles, with bindings intact, unread.

The second from the bottom shelf holds promise. It actually looks like the shelf is drilled to the back. I am wary. Can't tell if the bookcase is attached to the wall or free standing. I don't want an avalanche of dusty books knocking me unconscious.

I try to shake the bookcase a bit to test its solidness. Yep. Could work. I place one hand on the stack of books and the other on the desk leg and try to shove myself up. My book hand can't get a grip because the top book has a paper book cover on it. I take it down so I can grab the next book in the stack, and something drops on me. Heavy. I scream. Is it a giant grey bug? No, it is not. It is a key stuck under the book cover for safe keeping.

God is good. Bugs are not.

I let Betty try the key. The center drawer opens and there are keys of every shape and ancestry in the drawer. Wow. Berry collected antique keys, or they collected him. The drawer is also filled with bills. Some are unopen and some look in Spanish? In Haitian? Ok. What the heck?

I am concerned about the bills. Betty, did you pay all the bills this past year? Are those in the drawer paid? Betty looks whiter than her white. She points her dirty, long untrimmed fingernail at a bill. The bills are not addressed to this house. She does not recognize the address they were sent to. They are to Berry Johnson, but whose address are these? Oh crap. Berry. You devil. What. The. Hell?

I suggest to Betty that we get a box or two and empty all the desk drawers to sort out on a long table or clean stretch of floor. In agreement, we proceed to unlock the side drawers. Two of the deep drawers are easy. Berry's stash of alcohol is at least recognizable. The last drawer to the right is revolting. He had his candy and chocolates in it – totally covered with ants, alive and dead. This desk has to go straight to GOT-JUNK or whatever service they have in this small town. I am shivering up and down with the creepies.

On the other side is a drawer with neat hanging folders. Couple opened envelopes in the file folders…not immediately fascinating. Under this drawer is the bonanza. Checkbooks. A cursive glance indicates maybe three banks? You never know with banks merging all the time. But it is progress.

I have taken over the bill pile and am sorting them into months. Betty takes them and says no, sort them into utilities versus bank invoices. No matter. There are maybe about 25 bills. All to the same address. I ask Betty if this is Berry's office address. She says, oh no. Berry didn't have an office. He worked out of his home.

Beep, Beep, Beep. Back the bus up. He told me he worked in an office next to the mysterious Caribbean BBQ. I have a photo of his office desk with the cabinet of marathon running trophies in the background. We Face chatted or whatever it is called from his "office". I squeeze my eyes and bite my lip. Betty, I think we better find this address.

Betty looks at me with such discouragement and defeat. Oh God, I am so sorry. What did I do and who exactly did I do it with? I grab a pen and write on my hand. Get Dr. appt for STI (sexually transmitted infection). Now, I know you think I should be able to remember this on a "mental list". Well, my mental list days are 20 years behind me. Even something as important as see a doctor. Get checked for sexually transmitted infections. It will fall off my radar. Welcome to my world.

Betty puts one of the dogs in a large cage. Guess he is one of the old ones Berry worried about. With all there is to do around here, cleaning dog poo accidents is too much. Really, this is all too much and how Betty has made it this long alone, absolutely frightens me.

I enter the address from one of the bills into my cell for directions. I have grabbed all the keys and dumped them in a disposable dog poop bag I always carry. (I use them for soiled underwear if you must know). The address is about 4 miles from the house. The closest address is a hideous but "authentic" lean-to restaurant that boasts the cook is from Jimmy Buffet's. There are no office buildings next door, across the street, east, west, south, north.

The next reasonable possibility is nearby a storage unit rental place. Maybe Berry rented a room from the storage office building? It was closed.

I am worried that Berry may have an actual office that needs cleaning out. One that bills came to and are piling up? Did he pay rent on his "office" by the month or when he didn't pay was his stuff discarded? It has been just short of a year since he climaxed off the planet.

I sit with Betty in silence. I write down the storage unit name and phone number. Tomorrow is another day. We did a lot without making much progress. Let's get Betty back home and start a list of her priorities and compare it to my list of thoughts.

Betty remains silent. She walks all wobbly and crooked like me up her deck steps. I pause behind her at the door. I have not been invited in. Betty, do you want me to come in? No. Betty walks in and the sound of door latches snapping give me more than enough information.

I check in at my good ole motel off the pond. It is so strange to be back. I don't expect Barney Fife's girlfriend works here anymore. She's probably knocked up, planning her own baby shower, and still talking about her brush with fame.

No one recognizes me, my name, or my reputation. Everyone who is working is 18 years old and still talking about watching the fireworks in the back seat of one of those lifted trucks the boys drive around here. I am safe. And very tired.

I sit for a while in my room looking at the lake. I am plumb out of tears over Berry. I am so unbearably sad that I was so stupid and fell for his royal highness. Now sixty-three years old and still thinking someone will rescue me from my loneliness. I must pray for forgiveness because I have leaps of despair that consumes me. I have prayers of gratitude that Betty will let me help her. I pray petitions for God's plan be shown to me that I do the right thing.

I sit. In the stillness, when I thought there were no more tears, there are. God has the plan. I have a plain rubber bracelet in rainbow colors on my left wrist. God. Help Me. And it comes like a leaf falling unobserved from a tree.

Call Kristi, Betty's daughter. Betty is beyond grief. She appears in a major depressive episode. Although, no one would fault her for being depressed. This is beyond grieving, I do not know how long it has been going on but by the condition of the house, more than two weeks.

Betty looks so frail and with just a marked loss of energy. I do not know what her medical condition is, but I wonder if she has had that checked in the last year. Moreover, Betty's hygiene, grooming and appearance are so sad like she isn't taking care of herself.

Just think that within 30 minutes, we accomplished more than a year of her looking at the desk and wishing she could open it. Some might have taken a hammer and broke the old musty desk apart rather than be immobilized. I want her daughter to know.

I went on Facebook to try and messenger Kristi.

Hi Kristi.

I am with your mom, and she is worrying me. Can you please call me?

Pepper

Not being a Facebook expert, I think I have to wait for Kristi to accept my friend request and then she might respond. Long shot.

I should have asked Betty for Kristi's phone number, but God just now told me what to do so I will keep hammering away to make it work.

It wasn't long before the blessing of Kristi's response comes through.

WTF Bitch. Why are you fucking with my mom?

I sense anger. I am psychic like that. God, please give me the words that Kristi needs to hear. I text:

Kristi,

You are right. It is unbelievable, but I am here in Dublin trying to help your mom. Can we talk please on the phone, I am concerned and that's why I flew down here. Seeing her today has me really wanting to help more.

Help me, help her. Please?

Pepper @ 651-486-2970

Kristi called. I braced myself for hostile. Nope. Didn't brace myself enough.

Daddy's little princess was beyond white rage. What is hotter than white?

Explosive dust?

I listened. Inserted lots of "you are right", "I agree", "totally understandable", "justified".

When Kristi's epic rant was winding down, I asked when the last time was that she saw her mom. Turned out it was three days after Berry had escaped his many parallel universes.

She was still mad at her mom for not pressing charges on me, the murderer. No arguing there. I had ridden the edge of being charged with murder for way too many months. But for the grace of God, it did not happen.

I inserted when she took a breath, "How soon can you come to Dublin?"

Kristi spit back, "Why the fuck do I want to do that?"

"Because your mom is sick. I just met her, but things are not right for any number of reasons."

Kristi seethed, "Yah. Because you fucked up our family."

"Yep. I did. But I do not want to see your mom suffer when something might help."

"Well, I just can't get away" Kristi said indignantly.

"Can I drive your mom up to you so she can get to a doctor and start getting better?

"No. Her doctor is in Savanah." Kristi was attempting an impasse, but I am a Professional.

"Great – can you please bring her to her doctor? I don't think she will work with me on it."

"You are an unbelievable asshole to try and guilt me. You whore." Anger will get you nowhere with a therapist, Kristi. Despite your inflammatory attempts.

"Okay Kristi. I am going to let you go. Please think on it. Sooner the better. Tomorrow before noon would be great. Thank you." I gently pressed end call.

Thanks God. That went well. Where is a Dairy Queen in Dublin?

Therapy Session: Bruce

Quick Recap:

Bruce is 70 years old. He looks his age and is appropriately dressed. He has an aura of pride I sensed from his first visit. Not haughty. Factual pride. Bruce has been married twice. Widowed once and divorced once. His complains are of a general disappointment in life and unhappiness.

Session:

Bruce is one of my toughest clients. I have a list of reasons why that is, and most are really about me. And therapy should really be about the client. That is a truth. And the judgers out there may deny this happens to them, but I am being real. I get scared, intimidated, shy, fearful sometimes in a therapy session. Although I joke that I am a Professional, I am also a person.

I am aware that I am uncomfortable with Bruce. As with most of our sessions, I sense Bruce is seething. He denies it when asked directly. He is smart and sees the question when I re-massage it and ask again.

However, my sense is that life happened with or without Bruce's permission. He was dating someone for seven years and she became pregnant. He was 28 and wanted to marry her and be the dad. She told him the baby wasn't his. He had had no clue she was seeing someone else. She broke up with him, aborted the baby and disappeared. Over the years he has tried to locate her but with no luck.

He fell in love again, married and lost his wife of 15 years in a car accident. Totally out of his control. Again. He did seven years of grief work, fell in love with the grief group leader and married.

That relationship ended when a 20-year-old showed up at their lovely suburban home and called Bruce "dad". Someone Bruce had slept with along the way had gotten pregnant. If you do the math, the young pregnant girlfriend had not been the only unfaithful one. The young man moved in "to get to know his dad better", managed within a week to get a $10,000 "loan for college" and a car out of Bruce. New son then drove the car and money away, never to be heard from again. Wife #2 was furious and left. Bruce views this as out of his control.

Me: Bruce, what would you like to discuss today?

Bruce: I don't really know why I am here. I really don't think this therapy is doing anything for me.

Me: What would you like the therapy to do for you?

Bruce: Make me happy, help me figure out things.

Me: Where do you want to start today then?

Bruce: I don't know. Give me some choices.

Me: Great. Sure. Let's start with your homework. What is on your list of 10 things that bring you pleasure?

Bruce: Oh yeah. Well, that didn't work for me. I know what I like, so it didn't make sense to waste our time here talking about it.

If you are still awake, you may feel frustrated by Bruce. That is a natural reaction to what is called "client resistance". Bruce is resisting the homework, expressing unrealistic expectations ("make me happy"), and not making any observable progress. Are you ready to blame Bruce? Or do you see the errors of my ways?

You may be right if you answered both Bruce and I are responsible. I will take responsibility for my part.

My responsibility:

1. I admit Bruce makes me uncomfortable. That "pride" atmospheric cloud impacts me negatively.

2. I find Bruce intimidating – I think he has a high IQ, and my guard is up less he find me a dullard and,

3. If he finds me a dullard, he will reject me.

4. If he rejects me, I will be hurt and the scar tissue over the gouge in my soul called "rejection" will be torn away. I will have rejection oozing over my carefully, band-aided life.

5. I personally feel no rapport with Bruce, so I am confident he feels no rapport to me.

6. No rapport, we are not building a therapeutic relationship.

7. Bruce is noncompliant with homework assignments. I must allow Bruce to create what he would like to work on between visits. I cannot offer assignments. If Bruce can't think of one, I must let this prescriptive stance of homework for all clients, go.

Bruce's responsibility:

1. Show up on time
2. Think about what he wants from therapy
3. Think about if he wants any changes or just wants to talk
4. Discuss the realism of someone else "making him happy"
5. Be open to questions about anger, self-sabotage, his core beliefs

I try again, after all, we have 47 minutes left to fill.

Me: Bruce, how do you feel about being given homework?

Bruce: Ok.

Me: On a scale of 0 to 10 with zero being not helpful and ten being of significant help, where do you feel homework assignments fall?

Bruce: Depends on the assignment.

Me: What number would you give if all the assignments are combined?

Bruce: I don't know.

The clock shows 45 minutes are left with Bruce staring at me waiting for the magic wand of wellness. Dang. Forgot to bring the wand today. I knew I forgot something. All I have is one last question.

Me: Bruce, what would you like to do for the next 44.5 minutes?

Are you interested in more information?

1. If you are thinking about therapy for yourself, there is a great article about how to prepare for Therapy. www.sonderwellness.com. See "Therapy 101: How to Prepare for Therapy. Great advice to set the stage for realistic expectations and the ability to maximize benefits.

2. What if you do not like your therapist? This happens. There are many reasons. The rule is that by the third visit if you are feeling the same way, seek someone else. You are unique and finding a fit doesn't always happen immediately. Therapists also sense poor fits with their clients, and it concerns them. If you are sensing a bad fit, google it! There are 31,600,000 results for "what if I don't like my therapist". You are not alone.

Chapter Sixteen

The next day I called the rental unit place. Fourteen-year male with cracking voice states "I never heard of him. We don't have a spare room to rent. We don't get his mail here."

I ask, showing flattering respect for a fourteen-year-old employee, "Sir, how long have you been working there?"

"Almost 2 months so I know you are wrong."

I press gently, "Is there anyone still working who was there a year ago?"

"Yeah. Comes in at 1 tomorrow."

"Name please?"

"Jeff."

"Thank you. Bye for now."

The mystery remains, but it occurred to me the post office might have a stack of undeliverable mail? I wonder if Betty could try to claim it. Maybe if she brought in a death certificate copy? Would be worth a try.

I thought of my naïve list of priorities. I was focused on getting Betty financially stable. After meeting her, she needs an infusion of mental health. And maybe a couple pots of coffee to ignite some energy?

I got to Betty's. It was really a pretty piece of property. I wanted to stroll around and touch the things Berry might have, but I didn't want to wash my fresh makeup away with tears. I knocked on the door. No answer. No dogs barking. Oh, maybe she took the dogs for a walk on paths I had seen winding through the acreage.

I sat myself down on the porch and drank Diet Coke and prayed. Every 5 or so minutes I knocked on the door and rang the doorbell. Both cars were in the driveway. Maybe she is showering. Maybe, she is in the laundry room. Maybe she walked to a neighbor's home. Maybe she is picking things in the garden. Maybe she is still sleeping, God bless her.

After about 45 minutes of playing the "maybe she is" game, I tested the doorknob. Locked. I walked around the house, courtesy of their amazing deck. Each door was locked.

Might there be a key under the mats or somewhere by each door? I slowed my roll and carefully checked. That neither dog barked was so strange. I knocked on windows – going to each window around the porch. Okay God. This is weird.

I braced myself and called Kristi. "Kristi, are you driving now?"

"No. Why?"

"I am at your mom's and the doors are locked, the dogs aren't barking, and Betty is not answering. Is there a spare key so I could unlock the door and check on her?"

"What the F? I am not telling my daddy's slut where the key is!"

"Ok. Then please come. This is not making sense."

I heard an exasperated sigh and click.

What now God? Call 911. It was a feather floating in my mind. Are you sure God? I still don't have my life together since the last 911 call.

I sat by the front door. God has the plan. My hands were shaking.

"911 operator. What is your emergency?"

"I am not sure it is an emergency, but do you do health and welfare checks?"

"Yes." Monotone voice. "What is the address? Please stay there and meet the officers.

Let me take your name and cell phone number."

I gave my name. Not a wince, giggle, blink. She intoned perfectly; "the police are on their way.

Do you want me to stay on the line?"

Oh, hell no. I am FINE. As in freaked out, insecure, neurotic, and emotional.

The police came with sirens and lights. A fire truck followed down the tiny dirt driveway. The ambulance pulled alongside the deck, spinning dust from its tires.

Barney Fife looking all of 19 years old now said, "what is the emergency?"

"Betty Johnson is inside I think, but she is not coming to the door. I assumed she wanted to meet this morning. Barney Fife snarls, "when did you last see her alive?"

I knew where he was going with the questions, but dear God, please let her be alive.

"Last night. I dropped her off on her porch at about 8:40. She went inside and locked the doors."

"Did you have an argument?"

"No."

"Do you have any reason to suspect she is ill?"

"Yes. She seemed frail yesterday, but it was the first time I met her, so I have nothing to compare it to. But something was off."

Barney sniffed like he had stepped in shit. At least it wasn't my shit. I was very constipated as flying does that to me. Barney asked his deputy, Office Clearasil, age 17, to try the door. Instead of knocking or ringing the doorbell, Clearasil stuck the butt of his rifle through the glass, and it nicked the wood door. Good job.

Barney snorted, went to a window, hit it with his rifle butt, shattered it and told Clearasil to climb in and unlock the door. I was horrified at the ineptness but mindful there was not one bark or whimper. Barney and Clearasil, clearly Dublin's butt brothers, went inside.

There they found Betty, staring at the television that had not been turned on.

She did not turn to see them. She was motionless. I stood in the room. Check to see if she is diabetic, I shouted at the EMT's whizzing by me. They put oxygen on her while they did her vitals.

"Come On. Check her blood level!" I insisted rather loudly.

"Why, is she a diabetic?"

"I don't know but she is acting like she is in a coma. But I have no medical history" I called back as I was dialing Kristi.

"Is your mother diabetic?" I said when she answered her phone. Krista in a dazed voice responded, "Yes, why?"

I left her on my cell and shouted over Barney's voice. He was arguing with Clearasil's whines that he had been cut with the window glass.

"She is diabetic!"

They proceeded to slowly prepare to take her blood. Poke her, damn it! I yelled in my mind. Good grief. I am slowed by arthritic and stenosis and yet I could have done it in half the time these yahoos were doing it.

Luckily, one EMT was calling someone. Someone at the hospital? To a grownup? They relayed her symptoms and her vitals. Betty was on a gurney very shortly after that and was on her way somewhere.

I asked, "Where are they taking her?" Barney extolled something inaudible. Good grief. What did you just drawl at me? Whatever it was, I could not hear clearly enough to discern. Maybe it was the thunder in my ears from stress.

I decided to look for the dogs. I forgot Kristi was still on my phone. The dogs were nowhere in the house. I was torn between checking on their welfare and trying to get to Betty wherever they took her.

Betty won over the dogs. Sorry dog lovers, but a comatose woman can't advocate for herself. I looked quickly to locate her purse, finding it, I stole it off the counter. Betty would need ID and medical cards.

I left her house open because the fine officers of the law where gazing at Berry's gun cabinet longingly. My pa had a blah blah blah...good grief. Hope they were above stealing from the citizens.

While I was in my rental car driving, I heard "bitch, bitch, bitch" faintly in the background. I knew it wasn't God talking to me. What? Was my blue tooth calling me a bitch?

Oh, I remember. Miss Manners herself was screaming at me to get back on my cell. I gently and calmly asked Kristi, "where do ambulances take people?" She screamed, "what ambulance?" I said, "You must come now. You can still be here before 1:00." And I hung up quickly, less my Bluetooth kept blasting "bitch" over Andrea Bocelli's baritone on the radio.

Betty received a recovery dose of something in the ambulance and she was groggy but alive. I was so happy to see her I took her bony hand and held it to my heart. "Kristi is on her way from Atlanta. Everything is going to be okay." Betty nodded and let me keep her hand.

Around 1:30, Kristi, the beloved one who speaks with grace and dignity, joined us in Betty's room. I happened to still be speaking softly to Betty it will be ok, God has the plan, you are loved, all will be well, all will be as it should be...just an impromptu mantra that seemed to calm her down.

She was so sleepy, but her blood sugar was on a monitor along with a fluid drip for hydration and a heart monitor and blood pressure leg cuff. Earlier I had asked the pimply doctor to evaluate for depression because she met the criteria of depression. The 22-year-old resident looked at me and said while it is possible that Betty is depressed, she is elderly, and her diabetes had been mismanaged thus mimicking the symptoms of depression that I was citing. Yes sir. My kids and one of my granddaughters are older than you, so be respectful. I may not be a M.D. goddess, but I do have a Ph.D. and am a licensed professional.

And that is as close to fuck you as I can get. Honestly. What I needed was the daughter's foul mouth tongue whipping this sap. When he starts shaving, he can maybe, possibly discuss with me that I do not know depression when I see it. Not until then. Jeez, have his balls even descended yet? Oops. Sorry. I am a professional.

At any rate, Kristi commanded the room and, as I felt her sucking out all the oxygen, I excused myself. I had been wearing a soggy diaper for hours. Time for a break.

Kristi, despite her serious lack of vocabulary and couth, had been gorgeous at one time. I had stalked her Facebook page before Berry passed and thought she was a Miss America. Tall, generous rack, skin like milk chocolate, Diet Coke colored eyes (no compliment could beat being positively compared to Diet Coke) and the perfect nose and mouth. Her hair was long and in soft spirals, tinted a Caribbean sunset blond. Berry and Betty had made an absolute Barbie Doll. A Barbie Doll without a soul apparently, because I kinda thought since I saved her mother from slipping into a coma death, she might lighten her tone to me.

I must extend understanding and tolerance. Kristi was now easily 120 + pounds heavier than a year ago. She was wearing the current style, expensively bejeweled, perfectly manicured. Certainly, she must be a fellow stress eater. I can relate. I am a compulsive overeater and the only reason I am probably not 300+ pounds is that when I am not constipated, I have a 24-hour episode of diarrhea. I added Kristi to my prayer list of intentions. So sad, so young, so much potential.

The next day, Betty went home, looking at least 30% stronger and better. I made a follow-up appointment with her personal physician and had to beg Kristi to take her. I had to get back to Minnesota. I am the parent for my Littles, and I honor the judge's decision to bestow their best interests in my care.

Kristi had been horrific to me, but I was thinking she might be unpacking venom she had stored up for the past year. I would extend her grace. And give Berry kudos for putting up with this brat. Wow.

Berry had been dead 1 year and 2 days when I flew back to Minnesota. I know I had left thousands of tangled webs (lots of them under that damn desk) but I had to earn money too and had a book deadline. I asked God what the next plan would be. Still have not heard. So, I make lists and keep lifting my heavy numb right foot in front of my heavy numb left foot. I just want you to know once upon a time, for 12 glorious hours, nothing was dead. But that seems like ages ago.

Time has changed things. I cry so easily now. I must have the thinnest scar tissue over some of the deepest psychic wounds. If I feel this way, my mind aches for what hurts Betty. So much unfinished business. And all of it in the very capable hands of Daddy's princess.

After the object of her hate left (me), Kristi mobilized around her mother, monitoring her blood sugar and nutrition. Betty wrote me they never found Berry's office nor did the post office still have any unclaimed mail. Kristi is organizing the bank accounts and trying to clear the house of 30 years of junk to prepare for a sale. Betty wants to live in a senior home that has graduated medical services. That will be expensive. The property will not net much as Berry had two mortgages on it.

I suggested that they contact Mari M and figure out whose name the Haiti plantation was in. They did. Berry had it all in Mari's name. Every bill, every everything including the girls who did not carry their daddies' last name. However, he did love them and richly blessed them financially. Berry left Mari a $5 million dollar life insurance policy. He provided well for his parallel universe.

Betty and Kristi never found any life insurance policy. Berry's Will was 20 years old, so inheriting cars that didn't exist wasn't much help. Betty owned the house, the acreage, Berry's 12-year-old truck, some antique guns, tons of dusty, boring looking books. She also owns one home mortgage and a giant home equity loan and a $1000 left on her car to pay. As Betty explained, they went to Europe once a year and travelled all over the United States. Kristi 's college was paid in full. That and 42 years of being happy and treated royally. It was saintly of Betty to keep remembering this, despite the worst year any woman can imagine.

The three parallel universes – or at least the three that we know Berry lived in – were built on lies. The more we explore, the more untruths are uncovered. Knowledge is not setting us free. It is entrapping us further in despair, fostering a mistrust of others, of ourselves. How could we be duped so colossally? We are certainly doubting and mistrustful of others to a much greater extent now. But we are more devastated to learn that we cannot trust ourselves.

In "The Voice of Wisdom" by Don Miguel Ruiz, there is a profound version of the Tree of Knowledge that I think may offer some healing for all of us living parallel universes. Remember the Adam and Eve story of life in the Garden of Eden? Life is wonderful and Adam and Eve and God interact with great love, kindness, and respect. One day, a serpent tempts Eve to eat an apple from the Tree of Knowledge. This Tree was also referred to as the Tree of Death. It was a glorious tree whose fruit was juicy and inviting. God had warned Adam and Eve that despite the beauty, this tree's fruit could cause death.

For in the Tree of Knowledge was a big snake, whose every cell contained poison. The snake was actually a fallen angel who no longer delivered messages from God of truth and love. Rather the message was of fear, not love. The message was a lie, not truth. When Eve ate an apple from the tree, it was because the snake of lies, lied to her. Eve was seduced by lies. As she consumed the lies, the lies consumed her.

The lies grew inside Eve and Adam like a tree. We are walking Trees of Knowledge, but the knowledge is all lies. The initial name of the tree was the Tree of Death. Truth died when we ate the apple.

Living in parallel universes, thinking that we can handle a little cyber flirting with a married person, is a lie. We are seduced by the beauty of it, but the beauty is a lie. What we tell ourselves to justify our behavior is a lie. When we move the line in the sand to accommodate our feelings, we are lying.

I take responsibility for living a lie for a year. I lie when I think I am better for having had Berry. I am not seeing the truth when I cling to my photo album. The truth is, I embrace the lie and don't have what it takes to embrace the truth. Unless that too is a lie.

I am a professional. Despite this, I still keep Berry's photo album under my pillow. At around 2 am every night, I'll turn on my cell flashlight, open my album and touch the picture of his bare chest. And gaze at his dick pics. Will I ever be able to give up the lie? The only truth I know is that God has the plan.

Last Chapter (I Promise)

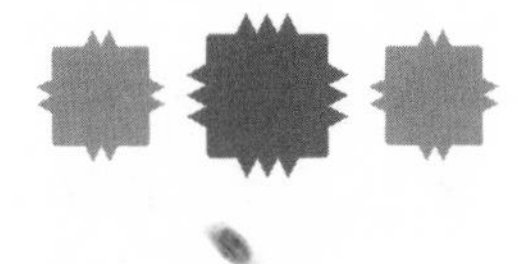

I know you care about my clients* and are probably curious where they are today. Here is the latest update:

Jack & Diane – Diane experienced some positive changes in her life. Diane found two volunteer jobs that can be done from home. One job is Love Letters. Great organization spreading hope, caring and comfort through letter writing. Their website is www.moreloveletters.com. Diane also discovered crocheting plastic bags into mats for homeless persons. The website is: https://love-crochet.com/crocheting-plastic-bags-for-the-homeless. (Check your State for distribution.)

Jack left therapy not reporting any changes and frankly spat that he never did understand the point of therapy. Oh well, win some, lose some!

Ed & Eddie – It is very exciting to report that this couple enjoyed a European vacation and came home to build their family through the foster-to-adopt program in their state. They are waiting for their Home Study to be completed. As a couple they continue to see me once a month. In between this session Eddie comes twice a month and Ed comes once a month. They are doing well and enjoying their lives! No need to inhale a Dairy Queen after their sessions!

Jerry & Janice – Something positive happened after something bad. Jerry was diagnosed with diabetes – something bad. Jerry took the diagnosis seriously and quit drinking, successfully sustaining sobriety! Janice supported his sobriety by becoming sober herself! They continue to see me twice a month and we are making great progress. There is a lilt to their teasing each other. Their favorite expression to each other is, "you married It". Think about it. Hilarious, right?

Dan & Darlene – Probably one of the most dramatic therapy results to report. Dan lost his job due to "downsizing" which unfortunately sounded very much like age-discrimination. He had divorced Darlene prior to his dismissal and is required to pay significant alimony despite his joblessness. Darlene is in Europe enjoying herself immensely.

Dan schedules sporadic appointments. Darlene has not been seen again and I would not call her a therapy drop out because according to Dan she is living the dream on Lake Como in Italy!

Amy, ahh…Amy – Amy is still seeking a new position at work. Every day she is vulnerable to being fired if only Human Resources would allow executions over personality conflicts.

Amy continues her weekly visits and recently has gained some insight. A new mantra she has embraced: Flattery will get you everywhere because I have such low self-esteem. Hopefully this mantra pops into mind on a Saturday night when a lonesome stranger begins a slew of road-hard pick-up lines!

Ben & Barbie – The marriage of Ben and Barbie, as you probably predicted, did not survive. Ben has an apartment. He remains close to his teenage child. Barbie is still employed by the same company but has been reprimanded twice for having pornographic images on her computer.

Barbie sees me faithfully once a week. She has a lot of sexual repression steaming out like a dragon with 10 heads. Ben did not return to therapy, and my hope is that he finds contentment and peace and a woman who can appreciate the power in puny.

Kramer – Kramer experienced drastic changes! Not from my therapeutic excellence. He was shot in the thigh by a fellow officer – he believes it was by accident. Mmm... He is on administrative duty now and considering a career change. I see him every week and we work on his career transition. Kramer and I have actual conversations! He is a stoic man that deserves the best.

Gladys graduated from therapy by leaving the planet, heaven-bound no doubt. A few weeks before she passed, she had sent a beautiful thank you note. I keep the note in my treasure chest.

Leslie, a truly resilient woman, lost her spouse not to cancer, but of a massive stroke. With his loss came of course, another economic hit as she is living just on her social security now. She still comes in whenever she needs to. Prayers are very much needed for this struggling client.

Olive – Exciting news to share about Olive! Olive connected with an adoption support group and made friends who understand her challenges. Olive joined Nutritional Weight and Wellness, www.weightandwellness.com, and stopped dieting. She is happy to report her weight is ok for her. Olive faithfully comes in once a month. I am happy to report that Olive's spouse remained the same. As such, the School of Natural Consequences failed him, and he is living in his parents' basement, blaming Olive's weight loss for the separation. I believe Olive lost 225+ pounds the day he moved out!

Pepper – My secret is out. My family doesn't look at me the same. And frankly, in the fashion of Rhett Butler, I don't give the d-word. I am a professional, don't you know!

Jesse – Jesse had a few more sessions with me before he came one day with his wife. His wife took one look at my short skirt and chubby uber-sexiness, and she left with Jesse meekly following. What can I say? I rock these 200 pounds!

Bruce – Bruce came three more times, accomplishing nothing. I explained that I was discontinuing taking his insurance. He looked damn relieved. I referred Bruce to his insurance's website to vet his next therapist-victim.

*Nationality, race, gender preferences, and gender identification were intentionally omitted as people who come for help share a universality of the majority of problems – power, money, time, love, lack of love and penises falling into vaginas or other orifices. I apologize if I did not address a specific issue. Please write me with your thoughts and do not include any pictures of your naughty bits.

Replies to Readers and Haters

Dear Avid Photographers of Your Own Junk,

I am in receipt of what you must deem as extraordinarily interesting and well formed. Sorry, but you have sent it to the wrong person. I am not impressed but grossed out. I had no idea how many amateur photographers of odd-shaped body parts there are. I recommend a therapist skilled in disgusting behaviors.

While I do not understand the CLOUD and how it can possibly keep such an array of revolting pictures for all eternity, I hope you will understand that there is no retraction after sending your personal pride out to the world. But I certainly am not keeping a single picture of your manhood. And ladies, I am not interested in your womanly bits either. But out there in the universe, those images are FOREVER.

And just to be clear – your picture did NOT go into my Berry photo album.

Sign me:

Once You've Had The Best

• • •

Dear Professionals,

While I admittedly do not receive criticism well at all, I am particularly offended by some of the less than professional treatment of a peer that I have received. You read my book. Thank you for doing so. You may have found the book in the FICTION department. FICTION is defined as creative writing. I wrote a FICTION book.

I will write slower so that you can keep up. Fiction means not factual. The clients, while written to appear real, are not real clients. My running dialogue is also FICTION. Yep. I made up the dialogue. I realize that you may also have a similar running dialogue in your head when seeing clients. Are you reacting to the fact that the mystery of being a therapist has been revealed? Is the emperor naked?

Please seek consultation on your feelings of nakedness. Please google FICTION to get a better perspective on my writing.

Thank you.

Sign me, Your Peer Who Wrote a FICTION novel, and you did not.

• • •

Dear Clients Engaged in Therapy,

First, I applaud you for engaging in therapy. I wish you nothing but positive changes and healing. Of the thousands of letters, I received and will continue to receive, I wish to repeat what I wrote at the beginning of this book. Not one single character is real. The problems brought to therapy are real but blended like a smoothie so there is not one single distinct taste of a vegetable left.

If you feel exposed, I apologize. There are millions of people wrestling with the few issues I highlighted. You are not alone. However, you are special. You are unique. But your issues are those of humanity. I recommend support groups to understand our similarities. I do not recommend reading fiction and identifying with a character so totally that you feel compelled to send hate mail.

Please use the 48-hour rule before responding from a point of angst. Blessings on your efforts at self-improvement. Clearly you are a work in progress.

Dr. Pepper James

• • •

Dear Men, Who Fear They Are My Berry,

Wow! How many Berrys are out there? Hundreds of men wrote, worried that I was outing them. I wonder how many more didn't write but are hiding my book from their female partners? Or from their mothers?

You all need a spanking- and I don't mean the kind you will enjoy. If you recognize your Berry behavior, stop immediately. You are irrevocably hurting your wife, partner, children, the children you spermed, but aren't aware of, and your mother.

Get yourself to therapy and get sorted out. Living a transparent, honest life is an easier, happier one. As for the women you are using –on their behalf, I despise your duplicitous behavior. I cried enough to fill a lake while writing this book. The grief and loss never ends. Are you aware there is a wake behind your big 627-horsepower motor? You are sending your passengers flying off the boat into a tidal wave.

And why? So, your penis can fall into a vagina. Get a grip of yourself, shake and release. It's safer that way.

Sign me: One life, one partner wearing a life vest at a time

Dear Men, Who Want to Be My Berry,

Thank you for your interest. It is not necessary to apply for the position with a picture of your junk looking happy. As I learned from Berry, he wanted his junk adored, whereas I wanted a real relationship.

Introducing your junk first tells me that you are not interest in me but have taken a perverse way of grossing out my secretary and publicist. Stop. Now.

Sign me: No Berry's Need Apply

• • •

Dear Berry Applicants that Applied with Dignity and Their Pants On,

Since the publication of this novel, I have received hundreds of applications to be my new Berry. As you know from the fairytale Cinderella, the prince was not looking for just anyone in the kingdom. There was a certain something about Cinderella that created the magic. The glass slipper didn't fit other women no matter how they tried.

Applying to be my Cinderfella is flattering but I am looking for the special one that fits the glass condom.

Sorry to disappoint you.

Princess Charming

• • •

Dear Family,

Okay, I can hear your collective Catholic gasp. Your daughter/sister had sex outside marriage. With a married man. She keeps pictures of a male appendage with her. She wrote flirtatious texts to a stranger. She spent eleven days stalking a man in his hometown.

Let me see, is that everything on the list for going to confession? I am sure not. However, I am able to keep my own list of sins to confess and my own tally of my failings. But thanks for offering.

I am sorry you are shocked, disappointed, but most likely, secretly pleased that I am such a screw up. I readily admit I am a sinner. Please enjoy your feelings of superiority.

See you at church, where I'll be first in line at the Confessional. Tip – get into the other line because I will be a while. I am bringing Father a Dairy Queen.

Peanut Butter Parfait Pepper

P.S. FICTION means imaginary as in I have a very dirty mind, that is all.

• • •

Dear Friends,

What can I say? You aren't in my book – not a trace.

Consider yourself lucky.

Chinchin!

Rum

Content Warning

This book references various tools to enhance a marriage/partnership. I hope you enjoy them and may experience a renewal of your relationship and an increase in your relationship satisfaction.

However, some marriages or relationships should not be preserved. Please read very carefully the following caveat.

If you are experiencing the following in your relationship, please seek safety. Some of you may be experiencing some of these signs and are hoping marriage tips and self-help books will resolve your issues. Nothing will. Seek safety, counseling, advice. Many individuals do not recognize UNTIL they are out of a situation, how dangerous it was to themselves and to their children.

5 Common Signs of Domestic Violence:

1. The Partner Exerts A Large Amount of Control.
2. The Partner Engages in Emotional and Verbal Abuse.
3. The Abused Partner Feels Trapped and Unhappy.
4. The Partner Shows A Lack of Respect for You.
5. The Abused Partner Gets Visible Injuries.

What behaviors belong in these signs?

- Calls you names or insults you or puts you down
- Prevents or discourages you from going to work or school or seeing family members or friends
- Tries to control how you spend money, where you go, what medicines you take or what you wear
- Acts jealous or possessive or constantly accuses you of being unfaithful
- Gets angry when drinking alcohol or using drugs
- Tries to control whether you can see a health care provider
- Threatens you with violence or a weapon
- Hits, kicks, shoves, slaps, chokes, or otherwise hurts you, your children, or your pets
- Forces you to have sex or engage in sexual acts against your will
- Blames you for his or her violent behavior or tells you that you deserve it
- Threatens to tell friends, family, colleagues, or community members your sexual orientation or gender identity

These behaviors are not the only ones. If you question what is happening, call someone or some agency to help you discern your risks. Domestic Violence isn't only between married people. The more accurate term for domestic violence is Intimate Partner Violence. Violence of this nature occurs with any gender, across all socio-economic levels, spans all sexual preferences, includes people from all manners of careers and education, all races, all religions, all ages, and all cultures.

- For more information, please call 911 or the National Domestic Violence Hotline at **1-800-799-SAFE** or visit **www.TheHotline.org.**